woodsmoke

woodsmoke

BY SUSAN SIBLEY

JOHN F. BLAIR, *Publisher*
Winston-Salem, North Carolina

Copyright © 1977 by JOHN F. BLAIR, Publisher
Library of Congress Catalog
Card Number: 76-53744
ISBN 0-910244-93-6
All rights reserved
Printed in the United States of America
by Heritage Printers, Inc.
Charlotte, North Carolina

Library of Congress Cataloging in Publication Data

Sibley, Susan.
  Woodsmoke.

  I. Title.
PZ4.S56364Wo   [PS3569.I26]   813'.5'4   76-53744
  ISBN 0-910244-93-6

To M. K.

part one

Thy rod and thy staff they comfort me.

PSALMS 23:4

one

THE SUMMER
had been hot and dry, and the Carolina soil was baked out,
yielding little. H. A. Kieffer lived on tomatoes and sticky
Milky Ways that Thomas was tired of chewing. Jee Paw
carried around his Pepsi bottle, topped by a nipple. He
sucked haphazardly at it all day, his blistered lip sore and
extended. When the last ounce was gone and the air whistled
and whooed in the empty bottle, he looked under the orange
crate supporting the back step, found another one, opened
it himself, and transferred the nipple. "He's a bright little
boy for three," H. A. told anyone who would listen, and he
was proud of him.

H. A. was proud of all his family: Jee Paw, Thomas,
Elizabeth Ann, even Jenny Sue, who caused him so much
trouble. And Viyella, his mother. All of them, except Jimmy,
his father. But he put that out of his mind.

The dirt yard was swept clean; H. A. saw to that now
that Viyella was laid up and Jimmy had gone, but dust blew
around on it anyway, swirling, never settling. And Thomas
was tied with an old piece of clothesline, snug under the
chinaberry tree, watching the wind chase the clouds across
the sky. It promised rain, but no rain came. The earth was
thirsty, parched raw. There were cracks in the ground wide
enough for Elizabeth Ann's hand. She could line up her stick
dolls in them, straight up, two by two. Jenny Sue, peering
down, thought she could see clear to China and planned
to dig to China with Viyella's stewing spoon, but H. A.
knew she never would have the patience for that. She never
had the patience for much of anything except looking at
herself in the broken mirror of Jimmy's car when he brought
it home. She simpered and cocked her head to one side,

and her little feet hopped up and down, dancing in the sand.

The Kieffers lived far out on the highway, eastward towards the coast, just before Shem Baker's gas station and beyond the Bloody Bucket, where even by midafternoon cars drew up in the pitted, potholed parking space. The jarring sounds of the jukebox and the voices and laughter rising blared out over the quiet countryside, drowning out the cardinals, orioles, and even the blue jays fussing and arguing among themselves. Just beyond the tavern there was a narrow, rutted, sandy road. And down that road, around the bend by a big pine, was their house, hunched down on crumbling brick stilts. There wasn't any porch (Jimmy never got around to building one) but the orange crate backed up against the door where H. A. kept the Pepsi Cola for Jee Paw, filling it bottle by bottle to keep Jenny Sue from getting any. She was big enough to fend for herself, but Jee Paw was the baby. Until the new one was born anyways, and that would be soon, any minute most likely.

The orange crate did for a step and was a good spot for Jimmy to sit of an evening to smoke his cigar while Viyella did her dishes, standing at the kitchen sink and watching the sun go down.

H. A. sat on it now, scowling as he glanced worriedly across the baked field. Beyond the row of pines, the swamp, the marshy woods, was Mrs. Parker's place. He strained his brown eyes against the hot sun, as if seeing the house might bring it nearer somehow. The time was coming to go get her to help, because Viyella wasn't doing her dishes now, or chasing Jee Paw or singing to Thomas, or hanging out the clothes to brighten in the sun. She was prone on her iron bed, sweating under her quilts in the August heat, but cold just the same, cold through to her thin bones, the back of her neck clammy.

Could birth her himself maybe, H. A. thought. He had

4

helped before, but his arm wasn't coming on the way it should. He could hardly slice the tomatoes or stir up the grits, could hardly lift the arm at all any more. His boil had seemed to inch right down his shoulder. Fascinated, he examined it every day. It had a life of its own, and sometimes, red and yellow and black, it seemed to be roaring at him, calling his attention. Other times, it was still and sullen. The mud packs he put on, when he had the time and no one was looking, might be cool and comforting, but they weren't doing much good. When he scraped them off, the boil was still fierce, angrier than before.

Sometimes when Jee Paw tugged at him and touched his arm by mistake, H. A. cried out. But usually he bit his lip, and his tears dried quickly in the hot sun.

Then Jenny Sue hit him there on purpose.

"You do that again and I'm going to have to lick you."

"You wouldn't dare!" She squinted her eyes and made the face he hated, her little pink tongue wiggling between her lips, mocking him.

"Jenny Sue, listen here. Ma is like to die and Daddy is gone. Help me, please."

"Think you're big stuff, don't you, H. A.? Biggety!" She put her hands on her hips and jutted her chin out. "Who made *you* the boss?"

H. A. took a switch to her then, cringing more than she as the welts rose up on her skinny legs like the corduroy ridges of his best pants.

"Reckon I'm head of the family now," he said. "Jenny Sue, mind. Please. I don't want to hurt you." He went easy, but Jenny Sue howled anyway. "Hush," he whispered. "Hush!" he commanded, raising his good arm, threatening her to silence.

"What's that? What happened?" Viyella cried from where she lay, buried under all the quilts H. A. had been able to find.

"Don't fret, Ma."

Jenny Sue's whining faded to a whimper, and H. A. warned her again, but there was no need. Inside, Viyella sighed, and her voice trailed away like a wisp of smoke before he had even finished.

Yes, the time was coming to get help; H. A. was sure of that. But how to do it? Whom to send? Couldn't go himself and leave his Ma. Who would tend her? What if she screamed? Jenny Sue would only run and cover her ears. She was so spoiled she was just about useless. People were always talking about her, with her right there pretending not to listen. She would get that little smile on her mouth, not a happy one, just pleased with herself, as if she knew a secret.

"What long black lashes," women said, "and with that hair too!"

Jenny Sue's hair was the color of milk; you could hardly tell it from her skin.

"What a little sweetheart," men said. "C'mere sugar," and they patted her head and smoothed her hair and twisted it into curls. Her father was the worst of all. Now Jenny Sue didn't think she had to do what anyone said, especially not H. A., since she was nearly as old as he.

But he couldn't send any of the others. They were too little, and they wouldn't know the way through the swamp. Jee Paw might remember the message, but in places the muck was so deep it'd be up to the cowlick standing at the back of his head. Thomas would forget; he wouldn't mean to; he'd just wander off listening to the stillness, hearing sounds beneath and following, till he was lost. Elizabeth Ann was so scared of the dark he couldn't send her there, with not a strip of sunlight slanting through, not a bright patch anywhere. All black it was in that swamp. And he couldn't count on any of them to watch out before they set a foot down. He had forbidden them to play there, ever, because of snakes. Cottonmouths lay still as logs in the shadows, hidden in the Spanish moss that dripped from the white oak trees and touched one's face like a spider's web. And moccasins skimmed along under the dark pools of water, lurking in the roots of the cyprus. H. A. shuddered.

He glanced again across the field shimmering in the heat, but Mrs. Parker's house was still hidden behind the wall of pines, no nearer, no matter how he frowned. He squinted down the road, shading his eyes, but no one was coming. He expected no one.

Jimmy had disappeared five days ago, and the neighbor women had gone home to tend to their own affairs. They said they'd be back, that it would be a long time coming and everything would be all right. But everything wasn't all right. The baby was stuck. H. A. knew, because with the last one, the puny one that died, it had been the same way, with his Ma lost under her quilts, too tired even to holler like she did with Jee Paw. But the County Nurse had been there then and had taken over. His Daddy had refused to ask her in again. "No woman's going to fuss at me," he'd mumbled, shuffling about the house, doing useless things like lifting covers off the pots she'd set on to boil and swiping at flies. "Won't tell *me* what to do. Don't need no woman in; never did before."

Eventually her tongue had driven Jimmy from the house. "Ain't all my fault," he had protested, raising his head from the bed where he had buried his face, his bloodshot eyes, red from weeping and drink, looking everywhere but at the still mound under the quilts. "Ain't my fault. Man does what he can."

The door had creaked to behind him and he had ambled off down the road, raising small screens of dust when he kicked at stones in his path. By the time he'd come home, the County Nurse had gone and H. A. had buried the baby, in a shoe box Mrs. Parker had given him, under the pine tree whose branches swished and whispered against the house when the wind blew.

His boil was hurting bad now, getting worse. H. A. rolled up his sleeve, letting the sun beat on his arm. Mrs. Parker had scolded him, when she came before, for wearing his striped Sunday shirt. (He could still button it at the wrist then, before the boil swelled to the size of an apple.) "Who do you think you are?" she had snapped. "Your Daddy? Slicked up fit to kill." She had said he should be ashamed dressing up as if for church, just because his Ma was too sick to stop him, and when he had so much to do, him being head of the family. "A dandy," she had scorned, "just like Jimmy."

Maybe he should have let her see it, H. A. thought. But then what? She'd have packed him off to the clinic at the Marine Base, and what would have happened with him gone? No one understood that Elizabeth Ann had to be sung to at night, at that hour when the world turned blue and the woods softened into the sky and the train whistle mourned far off and she was lonely. No one knew where he hid the Pepsi Cola so Jenny Sue wouldn't get it all. And who would have had time to tie Thomas to the chinaberry tree so he wouldn't wander off, following the bird songs into the swamp?

And anyways, the mud always worked with bee stings. It just took a while, a little longer this time, was all. And soon his Daddy would be back, figuring it was over.

The scream came now as H. A. had always known it would sometime, had dreaded it, hearing it along his flesh and the back of his neck. He ran into Viyella's room, but when he bent over the bed, he couldn't hold her still. He tucked the covers around her shoulders and wiped her face with his shirt, pushing back the tangle of hair and murmuring, "Hush, hush." But his other arm hung useless at his side, and he knew the time had come.

He found Jenny Sue tickling Thomas with a pine branch and called her to him. "Jenny Sue," he warned. "You listen to me, every word." She stood before him, hopping first on one foot, and then the other.

"Can I have Jee Paw's cola if I do it? Can I?"

"Now mind. When you get to the woods, you walk careful. You watch every minute. Don't put your foot . . ."

"I won't go unless you promise, H. A. 'Lost my partner, skip to my Lou' " she sang in her biting little voice, and her hopping turned into a tiny dance in time with the song.

"Jenny Sue, stop that!" His good hand reached out and grabbed her shoulder, his fingers fastening tightly around the bone. "You want a moccasin to get you with his sly, mean mouth? You want him slithering out of the shadows, creeping over your ankle? Long, wavy, slimy snake. You want him biting at you between your toes so you won't never dance again? You want to swell up and turn black all over?"

She began to cry, her lips working, trembling, in the pitiful look that always melted her Daddy.

"I don't want to go, I don't . . ."

"You got to." H. A. was stern, still holding her fast.

"Then I get Jee Paw's cola?" She brightened.

"You get back here with Mrs. Parker. Then you get the cola, when you're back."

He watched her cross the field, a bright red flag (the new dress his Daddy had brought back with him last time) waving in the long grass. Soon she began to bob up and down and sideways.

"Jenny Sue," he called, his voice strained, sounding lonely and mournful like the train across the pine flats in the night. "Don't *do* that! Don't skip! *Please*, Jenny Sue. Watch where you're going!"

9

She stopped and turned at the edge of the field, too far away for him to tell for sure, but it looked as if she raised her hands to her head, and he guessed she was wiggling her fingers and sticking her tongue out in that ugly face she made at him when she was safely out of reach or behind Daddy's legs. Then she turned again and was lost in the dark of the woods.

I had to, didn't I? H. A. thought wearily. I had to. He sat on the step a minute longer, his shoulders slumped in defeat, his head on his knees. He waited for the tears to dry in the hot sun before going in to his mother.

Viyella lay quiet now in her old iron bed, helpless with pain, dragged out and dreading, weary and far away in her own thoughts. Her eyes were sunk deep in their hollow sockets, and she hardly saw H. A. when he came in, the hidden arm hanging limp at his side; but she knew all the same his familiar figure, his own stretched-out thinness. She worried over them all, but most over him starving himself for them, afraid he would stunt his growth in his quick-growing years. She didn't eat much herself any more and took scarcely more than rabbit bites of the grits he brought her now.

"Thank you, H. A.," she began, but her voice was so weak he could hardly hear it, and she wondered if she had spoken aloud. H. A. put his finger to his lips, shook his head, and then smiled at her.

"Shhh, Ma. Save your strength." For what's to come, was the unspoken thought that followed.

"Made of tears, I am," she murmured with disgust, as her eyes filled and water spilled down her cheeks. "Nothing but a sea of tears. H. A., you don't even need to season. I make everything salty enough." The tears had dripped into the grits. Viyella put the bowl away and lay back.

She moved her legs, and H. A. could almost see the pain

slicing up her middle, spreading sideways, gripping her under her ribs.

"The baby won't budge no further," she gasped. "I'm sorry, H. A. I can see your arm, big as a tree trunk now and hurting bad as me."

"No, Ma, hush," he said.

Slowly, with an effort, she raised up again, and carefully, guarding the pain, began to swing her legs around. Then she fell back, moaning.

"Where are Mrs. Parker and the others? Where is Jimmy? Oh, God!" she cried, "H. A.!" and then for a brief, blissful moment, she lost consciousness.

Where *was* Mrs. Parker? H. A. stared out the window. It seemed forever that Jenny Sue had been gone. Then at last she came into sight, limping so noticeably when he saw her that his heart nearly stopped in fear. But it was all right—it had to be.

At least Mrs. Parker was with her. Large-boned and brisk, she waited impatiently, one hand on her hip, the other on Jenny Sue's back as she none too gently urged her on.

"Hurry now; ain't so bad as all that. Step along." Her voice carried over the quiet fields.

Jenny Sue quit dragging her foot and stopped altogether, stubborn, but her whining, lost in a sudden groan from Viyella, was as reassuring as Mrs. Parker's blue-checked body and the large Economy shopping bag filled with the necessities she toted, coming along to make it right.

Can't be too bad, H. A. thought. Jenny Sue wouldn't fuss so. But he bit his lip down hard in worry, and only his mother's voice kept him from running out to meet them.

"H. A.," Viyella whispered. "Go on. Take care of your sore." Her eyes had cleared, and it was as if she could see right through his long-sleeved striped shirt to the ugly boil underneath. "Leave us be. We'll be fine. He'll be along directly. Fine." H. A. bent close to hear. "Take care of it, H. A. Ain't getting no better. Go on now."

"Ma, it's all right. When Mrs. Parker gets here, I'll go," he said. "Take ahold of my hands now, Ma."

But her eyes had clouded over, and she gave a long, shuddering sigh before she rose up, tortured; and H. A., forgetting, held her with both hands. His eyes stung as the pain, shooting through his arm, overwhelmed him.

What was taking so long? Couldn't Jenny Sue walk any more? Snakebite worked fast, he knew, speeding the poison along from the toes, up the legs, swelling, blackening as it went. Sweat gathered on his forehead and poured down his face. But I can't go out and carry her, he thought wildly, his arm on fire. Couldn't even pick up Jee Paw's cola bottle right now.

Viyella arched, the quilts tangled in her feet, and gently he lay across her, holding her safe.

"H. A.!" she screamed. "Oh, God Amighty! Oh, Lord Jesus!"

"Ma." His voice was as ragged as her old nightgown. "Hang on, hold!"

Mrs. Parker's firm step sounded on the orange crate, the old kitchen linoleum, and then she was there, Jenny Sue hobbling in behind her.

"I got bit by a snake," Jenny Sue piped shrilly. "I got bit by a shiny old—it was your fault, H. A.!"

Terrified, he turned to look at her, even as Mrs. Parker set her paper bag down and pushed him towards the door.

"Jenny Sue," he started.

"I did! I did!" She was pitiful, her red dress bedraggled and a twig caught in her long, milky hair. But Mrs. Parker didn't look.

"Out children, out," she ordered harshly. "Give your Ma some peace."

"I got bit," Jenny Sue repeated woefully.

12

"You hush, Jenny Sue, right now." Mrs. Parker was working all the time, laying out smooth, sun-white strips of cloth. She bent over to place firm hands on Viyella's heaving abdomen. "You ain't hurt, Jenny Sue. Now get out, the both of you. H. A., set the water on and then get you on down to that clinic. Hear?"

He went to do as she said, but Jenny Sue reached out and stopped him. "See H. A.?" she said. "See what . . ."

"Jenny Sue!" Mrs. Parker was angry. "Be quiet!"

"My little toe," Jenny Sue whimpered, but softly, as she scrambled to her feet and ducked out. "See?"

H. A. followed her to the kitchen and put the pots on.

"You'd be gone by now if you was," he said gruffly, busying himself at the stove, not daring to look at her dirt-streaked feet.

"I . . ."

"You quit that racket! Your poor Mama in there." Mrs. Parker stood in the doorway. "H. A., you know you've got to go right down that road and get you a ride to the Base. You're going to lose an arm, boy, or worse."

"H. A.'s arm gonna be cut. Doctor take a big knife slit-slat, maybe cut the arm off!" Her toe forgotten, Jenny Sue began to hop up and down with excitement.

Mrs. Parker advanced. "What makes you so hateful, a sweet little girl like you? H. A., go on now, boy," she said more kindly. "Go see about that boil. I'll care for your Ma."

He hesitated, and her voice sharpened. "Go on. Go on down to the clinic. Jenny Sue, you find Jee Paw and Thomas, hear? Toe or no toe. Go, H. A. You can help your Ma better when you're two-handed. She sure will need you mended."

So off he went, Jenny Sue making faces at his back, Mrs. Parker clanking the pans on the stove, and the awful sound of his mother following him down the road. He held his limp arm with tense fingers tight against his side, the striped shirt dampened now, soiled in the hot bright sun.

13

They punctured his boil with a long, shiny needle, his arm clamped rigidly in the nurses' hands. He cried out, he couldn't help it; but then, like a balloon bursting, the boil seemed to shrivel before his eyes. They bandaged it, gave him pills, and put him to bed in a cot lined up with the other cots in the mustard-brown hall. People bustled by on soft rubber heels, their voices hushed, like the wind whispering in the pines. Often they removed the bandage and put steaming hot cloths on his arm that burned like grease on a hot stove but then, somehow, brought relief. They gave him food, feeding him as if he was as little as Jee Paw, and more pills, but mostly he slept. It was all happening as if in a dream, and he could hardly recall it the next day: only a vague memory of sights and sounds like something seen through a window, people appearing and disappearing, and indistinct, murmuring noises.

In a few days he was well enough to go home. And by the time he came back, it was all over.

two

VIYELLA WOULD not look at her baby or touch him, would not hold him or croon to him. When Mrs. Parker first brought him in, she turned her head away; and when the woman persisted, coaxing, "Now Viyella, see, he's a strong little boy. Ain't no beauty but, well . . ." hesitating, "not everyone's perfect, not always. Heard him yell though, Vi, didn't you?"; then scolding, "You ought to be ashamed, ain't natural," Viyella buried her head under the quilts to smother the voice.

She did the same when she heard the baby cry, far off and faint, mewing like a lost kitten above the bustling sounds in the kitchen. Not even for H. A. would she change her mind.

"Ma," he said when he finally came home. His best shirt was cut at the shoulder, and a sterile white bandage wrapped his arm to the elbow. Below, his wrist was still swollen, but the color had faded and he moved his hand gingerly. It seemed to Viyella as if he'd been away for weeks, but it must have been only a few days. Dimly she remembered the voices and cries and confusion in the kitchen, a clanging background to the other more terrible noise searing her own throat.

But she'd lost track of time. The hours drifted by in the changing patterns of shadows cast by the pine branches on her bed, and the window that Jimmy had always meant to screen darkened unnoticed, so slowly that sometimes it frightened her, when she opened her eyes again, to see the sudden square of black.

"Ma," H. A. pleaded. "Please look at him. He's a cute little baby. His fingers are so tiny, and he has dinky fingernails no bigger than a speck of dust." But she turned her head away from H. A. too, watching instead the green needles brush the window frame. "Ma," H. A. touched her shoulder lightly, "he's even going to have brown eyes, darker than mine. He . . ."

"No! Don't!" Viyella cried. What baby was worth snakebite, H. A.'s boil, torn flesh and mind, and hatred? Who wants a baby that caused fear and pain and nearly killed H. A.?

Her shoulder twitched under his hand and she was weeping, the sounds as soft and pitiful as the new baby's. She turned her head away, clamping her eyes tight together as if to shut out the image of the baby as well as H. A.'s pleading face.

"H. A., I'm sorry. H. A.!" she called after him, feeling the emptiness of her shoulder where his hand had been, hearing the door shut softly behind him. "Come back."

But when he came the next time he didn't mention the baby, and neither did she.

"Get you anything, Ma? Cup of water? Cracker?"

Often he didn't talk at all but just sat hunched against the wall while she slept. It surprised her sometimes, when she awoke, to find him still there.

During those days slipping by uncounted, unmarked by Viyella, now and then she saw the top of Jee Paw's head outside the window, his cowlick like a paintbrush sticking up bravely at the back. There would be a wave of the Pepsi bottle, a wait, and another wave. And then he would disappear, the last to be seen of him his stalwart brush, upright.

"Ma," begged Jenny Sue, "let me fix your hair. Please. Let me play Beauty Store." Without waiting, she reached over and jabbed a comb into Viyella's hair. She began to tug, the comb stuck in the tangled strands. She pulled. "Fix it real nice, real pretty," she chattered, but Viyella yelled with the pain of roots tearing.

"Go away!" she cried, and Jenny Sue darted out, leaving the comb behind, the prongs digging deep in the golden head. Viyella lay there, letting the tears drip down her cheeks, and left the comb where it was.

Thomas came in to look at the cardinal. Viyella didn't know how he knew it was there, but he went right to the window so quietly the bird never moved. He stood a long while and then turned to smile at his mother. The bird flew off the branch and out of sight.

"Oh, Thomas, you scared him," Viyella chided.

His smile faded slowly, and he fingered the quilts, his head cocked on one side, listening as if to his bird songs; then his chin dropped on his ragged shirt. He waited for H. A. to come in and get him and didn't look at the window again. Neither did Viyella.

Elizabeth Ann did not come in at all. Viyella heard the scuffling noises outside the door, the foot rubbing on the worn linoleum, and once she saw a small hand, its fingers clasped tightly around the door jamb. She knew Elizabeth Ann was there, but did not call.

Where was the baby? Viyella wondered idly. It was gone; it must be gone. There were no hushes from the kitchen, no busy footsteps back and forth, no lusty yell of hunger. How was it being fed? They'd have taken him to Emerald, maybe. Huh! Even in her listlessness the scorn rose, like the medicine she choked down only to have it surge back up her throat. Emerald surely would have enough for two, she thought, and then some, the way she flaunted herself. But she'd never bother, not Emerald, never risk herself in giving, never chance losing her shape. Don't know what the Lord really had in mind, building women as He did, Viyella mused. But He surely was a man as they said. Emerald.

Viyella had never been able to decide if the imagining was worse than actually seeing Jimmy at the Bloody Bucket with Emerald. But when the wind was right and blew the haunting music over the fields with a faintly eerie sound and she could hear the rumblings of the heavy trailer trucks lumbering north on the highway, she could picture so well how he looked and what he was doing, his thumbs tucked arrogantly into the belt riding low on his narrow hips, a small suggestive grin twisting his mouth, and his blue eyes crinkled at the corners in a sly, knowing look. She could feel his square hands, rough and masculine, their fingers spread as if pressing *her* back, even though so rarely and routinely did he hold her any more.

Now she thought, as she often did, of Emerald and Jimmy walking home through the fields, with the moon lowering in the sky and silvering the pines, and she wondered what Jimmy said as he leaned close to whisper in Emerald's ear. Was he gentle, tenderly pushing back Emerald's dark hair the better to see her face streaked by moonlight? Or did he

17

pull her to his hard body, mashing her breasts against him, forcing his arms tight around her, while he gripped her hair by the handful with fingers strong like wire, jerking her chin up and her mouth to his? Or did he laugh, was he gay, his hand just resting companionably on her shoulder in friendship?

Maybe none of this was happening at all, Viyella admitted. Maybe he was sitting around, joking with the men as he licked the beer foam off his mouth with the tip of his tongue and a satisfied smacking of his lips.

Who would ever understand the torment she suffered, lying alone in the big iron bed, as she had so many nights before, her hands clenched, stomach gripped in pain, body and nerves an impossible knot, taut, intertwined with love and hate?

I'll kill her someday, Viyella thought. Someday I'll go down there with the slicing knife, and I'll plunge it right through those big breasts of hers straight to the heart. A woman like that has no shame at all.

Viyella couldn't even have the satisfaction of picturing Emerald as an old woman with cracked hands and cracked skin, gnarled and dry and neglected. Emerald would never live long alone and forgotten in a backwoods cabin. Or if she did, not a wrinkle would she have, preserved intact with no feelings, like a mannequin in the Economy window. What an advantage Emerald had. Not caring was the secret. Being unconcerned. She could do anything she wanted and it wouldn't be written in lines on her face.

How could Viyella compete against such a woman with her own sorry body, her misshapen clothes hanging off the bones of her shoulders like the tattered shirt flapping on Mrs. Parker's broomhandle scarecrow?

Not caring. Ha! Jimmy Kieffer, Viyella silently jeered, Emerald don't even care for you! Those kind never have a thought for anyone or anything but their own reflection in the mirror or the sly eyes of men and the jealous, hating looks of women.

But what if Emerald did care? What if she wanted to live with Jimmy? Not just play with him, tease him, but marry him, adding another inch back to her shoulders while she strutted and swaggered and smirked, lording it over Viyella when they met at the Economy. Even so, what of Jimmy? Viyella wondered. For him there'd always be another Emerald. Wouldn't there?

Where *was* Jimmy? Viyella's teeth gritted so tightly her jaw hurt. Probably off pleasuring himself with Emerald, the two of them enjoying the moment with no thought for tomorrow.

I'll kill her, thought Viyella.

Oh, but if she did and left Emerald lying on the dirty floor with blood gushing and staining the tight satin dress, her face for once drawn in anguish, her hair limp and stringy, the life going out of it, what would become of H. A.? And the others? And herself? She'd be led away by stern, unfriendly men, the knife still in her hands.

Viyella turned on the bed, her back to the window and the moonlight slanting in.

"Just the same I may do it," she said aloud. But no one heard.

The house was very quiet. They *had* taken the baby away, Viyella decided. Maybe he had died like the other. Maybe he had starved. But how could she have fed him? Her old bones were as flimsy as a spider's strings, the skin just barely covering them, stretched tighter than the sweaters Emerald wore. There wasn't anything left of her to give.

But where had the children gone to? Why wasn't Jenny Sue fussing out there? Viyella thought about it off and on as she watched a blue jay preen himself on the pine branch.

Then early one morning when the needles still glistened

with dew, she saw them go. H. A. was leading them, Thomas with his rope tied firmly around his waist, the others strung out in a line behind him, heading for the woods.

"H. A.!" she hollered, rising up on her knobby elbow, "the swamp!" But they kept going; H. A. hadn't heard her. She sank back again. There was nothing she could do about it.

And then the day came, as it had to, when Jimmy sauntered home. She heard his whistle from way around the bend, tuneless because it was many tunes, hollow in its bravery. " 'Sugar Candy' " sounded intermittently when his breath came too close for the blowing out and the pursed lips. Next, " 'Positive. Eliminate the negative,' " false notes echoing emptily down the long dusty road. " 'Knows she's gonna meet a friend' "; then " 'Candy, call my sugar . . .' "

What a catch Jimmy Kieffer had been. Viyella sighed, remembering. Folks had whispered that he could have had any girl he wanted, even some older women—anyone at all except Viyella Redfern. They had mooned after him as he strutted around in his tight jeans, slung low over his narrow hips, tossing the forelock of black hair out of his face, his blue eyes so alive, so sharp that she could feel them piercing right through her.

"Please, Viyella. Viyella honey," Jimmy had coaxed, leaning on an elbow, his chin propped in one hand, the other hand warm against her breast. They lay in the field, the long grass the color of her hair a shield around them, a soft, wavering wall when the wind blew gently. And looking up, all she could see was the blue sky and the deeper blue of Jimmy's eyes.

"No," she said. "No."

No one could believe it. Viyella Redfern was a pretty girl, if you liked that kind of thin looks. But so were Esther Mary, Josie, and Emerald (even though her blood was mixed). After they were married, most of the women in

20

the community watched and counted on their fingers, and Viyella laughed to see them do it. It was a full eleven and a half months after the wedding when H. A. was born.

Only time I had any sense, she thought, hearing the steps on the orange crate. Only time.

"A man gets feelings," Jimmy mumbled, sitting by her bed, his head hidden, sunk in his shoulders as if he didn't have a neck at all, his blurry blue eyes faded like his jeans.

But Viyella wouldn't give him the satisfaction of asking, feelings for whom? Etta in Warsaw, Bonnie Dee in Fayetteville, Emerald? She shut her eyes and lay there unmoving under her quilts.

"Didn't mean to leave you, darlin'. Just couldn't stand to see you suffering, hurting so. Hurt me too. Just couldn't stand it. Honey, Vi, honey." His hand reached out, stroked her damp forehead, then slid down her face. She stiffened under his touch but still didn't budge, closing her ears to his pleading. "Sweetheart, it was always you," he wheedled, his voice hoarse. "You know that, Vi. Remember how we— how it was? Lying right here in this very bed, looking out the window with the big old moon shining in, making your hair like gold." His fingers idled gently, caressing.

Her body lay rigid.

"How do you feel, honey? What if you and me—?" His hand snaked under the quilts and she thought, I ain't even going to bother telling him to go away. I'll just lay here.

Later the same afternoon, Viyella heard the children's voices, faintly carried on the wind, preceding them through the fields; then louder came the harsh grating sound of Jimmy.

"What the hell's going on here? H. A.! What you doing taking them kids into the swamp?"

Viyella raised herself slowly, carefully leaning on her elbow, to look out the window.

"Daddy!" shrieked Jenny Sue. "Daddy, Daddy! That mean old H. A. made me go! I got bit by a—"

"You did *not!* What I was doing was teaching them all to get along in the woods," H. A. explained seriously. " 'Case any one of them had to go again. Was wrong before; I see that now."

"Daddy, H. A. was hateful to me while you were gone. H. A. whomped me with a switch, and he only gave me one cola." Jenny Sue whimpered pathetically. Her sad little head was bent, the pale hair falling over her face as she looked up at her father through her long lashes. Her hand plucked his pants leg, her small fingers tightening on his jeans.

"H. A., what have I told you!" roared Jimmy. Then, "Hush, darlin'; hush, sugar. H. A., you don't never lay a switch or a hand on my little girl. You hear? Shh, sweetheart, Daddy's home. Everything's all right now."

"Made marks on my legs—see, Daddy?" Jenny Sue showed the scratches from the pucker brush and thorny holly; H. A.'s ridges had long since faded.

"H. A.! You done that? Boy, you get my strap and bring it right here to me. I'll show you what happens to boys picks on their little sisters! You get that strap now."

Viyella could feel the ominous quiet, could see the children's big scared eyes circling round the boy and the man, could hear Jimmy's heavy breathing. She lay still for a long moment, listening.

But when H. A. (because he *had* hit her) said, so quietly she could scarcely understand, "Yes, sir," Viyella threw off her quilts and ran into the yard.

Jimmy was struck dumb. He stopped dead still, his hand upraised. H. A. gaped too, but stood his ground.

"Jimmy Kieffer," was all she said, but in a voice so terrible Jenny Sue quit snuffling. Viyella stood there tottering, her nightgown falling off her gaunt body, her faded hair blowing wild. "Jimmy Kieffer," she said again, and somehow she managed to straighten up, stand tall, her eyes staring him down.

The wind whispered in the pine and the children moved, their voices beginning again. Jenny Sue hopped on one foot, then the other; Thomas saw a bird, Jee Paw headed for the orange crate, Elizabeth Ann reached out to take her hand, and H. A. caught Viyella as she fell.

So Viyella was up at last, but she moved slowly about her house in the days that followed, exhausted, and she was back in bed before the day was over. More often than not the bacon would burn on the stove because she'd had to lie down in the middle of cooking it, and her grits tasted like H. A.'s worn old shoes because she hadn't the strength to stir them enough. And she still didn't want the baby, no part of it, no matter where it was.

She lay on her bed, on top of the quilts to be handier if needed, mornings, afternoons, and evenings, struggling up only when a child called, or the smoke from sizzling food drifted in, or there were unexplained loud noises or dangerous thunder in the west. Lying there, her mind went blank as far as the baby was concerned. There was no baby. Her body still ached and her bones were taut, denying her, but she put it out of her mind. There wasn't any baby.

Her own Mama, Bessa Redfern, had always been up and in the fields right after the children were born, Viyella remembered, and she, Viyella, had been about her business directly too. Maybe this was something else? But no. Her Mama had never ailed a day in her life till the last. And besides, folks didn't ail when there was work to do, only when there wasn't. And work there surely was: dust in the corners, pans needing scouring, copper kettle turning green.

She sighed now, lying flat on her back, her stomach a cavity, and pondered on Jimmy. Ailing or not, you couldn't expect no man to stay at home when his wife turned her shoulder to him. Men weren't made for sickness, either having it or caring for it. Made them ugly because they couldn't tackle it head on, fix it like hammering a nail or mending a fence, and have it be done, finished. No. Sickness was like fog, mist over the swamp in the early morning. Couldn't pin it down, touch it, but it was there. Who could fault him? As soon hold the wind still as Jimmy Kieffer. So off he went to the Bucket. And Emerald.

And Viyella tossed restlessly on her bed. Throughout the long winter months, first she was up and then she was down. But there was no baby. And little peace.

three

IT WAS early April, and the Judas tree had budded and the dogwood was beginning to bloom like dainty lace in the dark pines when H. A. brought the baby home.

He knocked hesitantly on the kitchen door as if uncertain of his welcome and unsure even that this was his house. He stood there patiently with his burden in his arms and said nothing to his mother when she came. For a long time he looked at her, his eyes holding hers, no appeal, no questioning in them, just serious, studying her. She stared back as steadily and silently.

At last she opened the door and H. A. set his bundle in her arms. The baby was tightly wrapped in a ragged, pink blanket, and when she glanced down at the top of his head, she saw, through the faint tufts of fair hair, that the soft spot was a cavity, a hollow, and her eyes flew back to meet H. A.'s.

24

"It'll fill out, Ma," he said. They told me it would in a while."

Viyella nodded. She laid her cheek against the softness and felt the beat of the heart throbbing through the fragile skin. The rhythm seemed light and insecure, and she clutched him tighter.

"What's his name?" she asked, her voice quivering a little.

For the first time H. A. grinned. "He don't have any. We just call him Fella."

The "we" hurt Viyella, like the time she fell off her horse as a child and a sharp piney stump went through her side, and it was her fault. She had been heedless. Desperately she clutched her baby.

"Fella." She shifted him to her shoulder and gently touched her finger to the tip of his nose. "We could call him Woodrow after his grandfather," she said.

"Could." H. A. followed her through the kitchen into her room, where she straightened the quilts and laid the baby down, the better to see him. "Don't think it would do any good now. He's Fella."

Viyella bent over him and began to loosen the blanket.

"Ma!" H. A. cried sharply. He flung his hand out and caught her on her forearm. "Ma! Wait!"

She turned her head briefly, questioning, but her fingers were busy with the wrappings.

"Ma, there's something . . ."

But Viyella had turned back to her baby, and it was too late. There he lay, clean, with pink and white skin, his blue-veined, long-lashed eyelids closed in peace and sleep, his fat little arms doubled up, raised to the ceiling, the small fists clenched for protection. And when the blanket came off in her tender hand, there were the fat, healthy legs, the dimpled knees, the calves, ending in raw, puckered stumps. There were no feet.

Viyella stared in horror, and H. A. grabbed her arm.

Then she shook him loose and ran to the kitchen. He could hear her retching into the dishpan even as he covered the baby again with the blanket.

"O. K. Fella," he said, tucking it in. "O. K. She'll be back."

The baby stirred, and H. A. called, "Hey Ma, he's waking up. Come see his brown eyes."

Everywhere Viyella went, she took Fella. She couldn't bear to let him out of her sight; even late at night, as she sat in her rocker darning Jimmy's work shirts and letting down Jenny Sue's hems, the baby huddled in her lap and she worked around him.

"C'mon Vi," Jimmy would urge. "It's long past his bedtime. You'll spoil him that way."

But he was talking over the baby's head nestled against her breast, and Viyella went right on threading her needle and expertly working it in and out of the cloth.

"Ha!" chuckled Jimmy. "You might miss and prick him one!" He tried to get an answering laugh, but Viyella's eyes were on her quick fingers darting over the material or resting briefly on the fair hair of Fella's head.

"You're just making extra work for yourself," Jimmy said, exasperated. "Takes you longer that way. C'mon to bed."

"I'll be along," answered Viyella, and after he had stomped off, she paused a moment, and then rocking gently, she crooned her old songs to Fella.

When she boiled the wash in the big iron pot, she set Fella carefully in the shade, propping him up against the trunk of the pine tree, with Jenny Sue or Elizabeth Ann or Jee Paw to watch, along with her, to see he didn't topple over.

Jenny Sue sulked at first. "You like him better than us," she accused.

Viyella saw the trembling lips behind the pout and real tears shimmering in the pale eyes and was patient.

26

"Jenny Sue, it's just he ain't been here as long, that's all, and we have to be so careful. See, his head."

She put the baby in Jenny Sue's arms, still holding him tight herself. Fella looked up, gurgled, and socked Jenny Sue.

"Hey!" she cried, "That tickled. I'll help you take care of him, Ma."

"Thank you," said Viyella. But Jenny Sue soon became bored and went about her own business, jumping rope, hopping and skipping about the hard-baked dirt yard, and plaguing H. A. when she could.

Viyella wouldn't leave Fella alone with anyone anyway.

"Poor little Fella," whispered Elizabeth Ann. "No feets. He's got no feets."

"That's all right," Viyella answered defiantly. "He's fine. They'll grow."

"You'll see, they'll grow," she insisted later to the neighbor women and to Jimmy when he grumbled.

H. A. made a harness arrangement, and Viyella carried Fella on her back on endless trips to the woods and fields in search of herbs and leaves and grass for ointments. Tirelessly she rubbed the sap of pine on his stumps. She hammered holly berries to juice and tried that. She mixed swamp mud and magnolia leaves and made a poultice. She walked all over the neighborhood with Fella strapped to her shoulders, her head covered by an old bonnet against the heat, and returned, perspiration staining her old dress, tired and sunburned, footsore, but always hopeful.

People could laugh at her, call her crazy as Emerald did, snickering behind her falsely sympathetic face and smoothly manicured hands, but Viyella knew. Those feet would grow. Just as Fella's head had rounded out, flat now in only one small fluttering place. And just as everyone was wrong when they said his brains would always be soft. Fella was the smartest baby she'd ever had, Viyella told the women, being careful just the same her other children were out of earshot.

"Look at him," she'd say, "sitting up there so straight." She noticed, if no one else did, how his eyes, now bright and shining, took everything in and then softened, reflecting, like the deep, dark pools in the swamp. His feet would grow.

But in spite of everything she tried, the stumps remained red and shriveled. Viyella hid them with H. A.'s long woolly socks.

When the sticky, dripping heat of August came, Fella began to yank and pull and work the socks off. Then he reached and explored his stumps with fat, interested fingers. He could sit for hours, absorbed in his task, and Viyella allowed it, if no one was around. But the sight of the stumps disgusted Jimmy, and she had to rush to put Fella's socks back on when Jimmy came in.

"How can you let him do that?" Jimmy would ask, turning his back.

"All babies like to play with their toes; you know that."

"Toes." Jimmy's voice was a bitter reproof, and Viyella hung her head. It was true. It was her fault, a judgment on her. She vowed the feet would grow.

Sometimes Jimmy was kind—if the stumps were covered. He'd pinch Fella's round cheeks, working the little mouth into absurd positions that made even Viyella laugh, and the baby would chortle at the sound of their voices.

And sometimes he would bend over close to Fella and whistle, first on one side of him, then on the other. Fella's bright brown eyes would cut back and forth and he'd make birdlike noises in return. Jimmy would smile then and lightly squeeze his shoulder.

"Hey, Fella," he'd say. "What do you think of that? He's going to talk any day now," he'd add proudly. "How about that!"

As long as the stumps were covered.

But Fella grew quicker and more adept at removing his

socks. He made a game of it, holding them up, laughing, showing off. And he wept in anger and frustration when Viyella struggled them back on. The socks were hot and itchy in the summer dog days and began to cause a rash. With water cooled in the dark place under the house, Viyella bathed the stumps, over and over again.

Heart leaves she used, and tar salve, to soothe, but they were of no use for her own pain.

The pain of loving children was never sharp, outright, she thought. It was worse than birthing them. It was a terrible yearning, an unfulfilled longing; a wishing, a lonesomeness like the moan of the mourning dove, an ache, a hunger nothing would satisfy. Tears were of no account. Locked lips, a silent heart, the cry repressed, the baby clasped to the breast—nothing sufficed.

Viyella held her baby close and rocked far into the night, singing softly, her voice throbbing with sorrow.

> *What is that blood on the point of your knife?*
> *My son, now tell to me*
> *It is the blood of my old gray mare*
> *Who plowed the fields for me, me, me*
> *Who plowed the fields for me.**

"Poor Edward," she sighed. The other children crept in to crouch in the shadows, silent, listening. Viyella saw them and smiled and yearned for them all.

> *What will you say when your father comes home*
> *When he comes home from town?*
> *I'll set my foot in yonder boat*
> *And I'll sail the ocean round, round, round*
> *I'll sail the ocean round.*

*"Poor Edward," anonymous.

29

Even with her eyes closed, her lashes glittering in the lamplight with the useless tears, she could see that H. A.'s face was thinning out. His chin was firming, and there were hollows under his cheekbones. His head seemed too big for his shoulders and his legs too long for his body. The sounds he made, unguarded, croaked like frogs in the swamp. He was growing. He would leave, and she could no more stop him than she could cut down the honeysuckle vine by the side of the road.

When will you come back, my own dear son?
My son, now tell to me.
When the sun it sets in yonder sycamore tree
And that will never be, be, be
And that will never be.

Viyella's throat hurt, and she clung to her baby.

She grieved for them all: Elizabeth Ann with her sad, serious eyes, pensive and afraid; Thomas, humming along softly—he'd be hurt, buffeted and battered and never understood; and what trouble of her own making lay ahead for Jenny Sue, even now whispering, "You're in my *way*, H. A., you're in my way"?

And Jee Paw, bright, stubborn, gallant little heart, holding H. A.'s ragged jeans in tight fingers. Jee Paw without H. A.?

And Fella. His feet would never grow, never.

Viyella shivered. Where would they all go? For go they would, one by one.

And what then for Viyella?

30

four

JIMMY WAS
hammering with more vigor than skill. The flimsy crate
split, pieces flew in the air, and his oath shattered the early
Sunday morning peace. He was going to fix the steps.

Watching his progress, Viyella sat under the chinaberry
tree, Fella asleep in her lap, feeling the sharp morning cold
bite through her thin sweater, seeing the mist rise, slowly,
lazily off the fields. Every now and then her lids fluttered
closed and she sat in stillness, only wrapping Fella's blanket
more tightly around him against the damp.

"God damn it!" Jimmy roared. Viyella's eyes flew open,
and she was sure they could hear him all the way to New
Bern. "God-damn-it-to-hell-sweet-Jesus!" He had given his
thumb a mighty blow.

Fella began to whimper, and now, for a moment, Viyella
looked at her husband with perfect detachment. He was
shaking his arm, alternately biting on his thumb and holding
it out before his face, scowling at the damage wrought. It
was growing big as a cucumber.

"God-damn-it-to-hell-sweet-Jesus!" he repeated, chal-
lenging her.

"Beg pardon, Lord," she murmured to herself and the mist
and the chinaberry tree.

And as he hopped about, his shirttail flopping, one big
foot clonking the dirt, his face drawn in protest, Viyella
wondered what she had ever seen in this man. Now his
mouth turned down in an angry pout, and his dark eyebrows
pulled together, threatening. He looked about him accusing-
ly, as if insisting that he was a good husband, after all, only
trying to take care of his home and family, rising at the
crack of dawn to fix the step, even though he had been
out late last night. The injustice he felt was plain to see

in the set of his shoulders and his frantically waving arm.

I must have been feeble-minded, Viyella thought, watching his performance unmoved. Did I really feel anything, ever?

She tried to remember, to catch again and hold those feelings, vaporous and elusive as the morning mist.

She had lain awake last night, alone and fretful in the big iron bed, worried that Jimmy might fall in the fire ditch on his way home; worried that he might lie there, bruised and bleeding, until someone, Shem Baker maybe, chasing his ragged mongrels, discovered him with barking and sniffing and shouting. She had cried, imagining his torn and dirty shirt, Jimmy the dandy with caked mud on his face and sand matted in his dark curly hair. She had been afraid and frantic that it would be too late, far too late, and that Jimmy's last kiss would be the greedy tongue of a mangy hound dog licking the dried blood and grime off his face.

The worry and fear, and the scenes of Emerald flashing through her head, had speeded up quickly like the moving picture show at Gassetts when it broke down, showing Emerald everywhere: arms, legs, crawling hands, glistening lips, hair flung wildly back. Then, as if the projector had stalled completely, there had been the large close-up: Emerald's face lifted, her eyes half-shut, waiting for Jimmy's kiss.

Now, sitting under the chinaberry tree watching Jimmy, Viyella recalled the other feelings from so long ago. How, breathless and happy and excited, she had danced home from school each afternoon and had dreamed through supper, sighing, hardly conscious of Mama and Papa, answering their questions from far away. How she had hurried her homework to get to bed, where she could lie and ponder on Jimmy and the field of grass and see again that dark forelock of hair over his eyes. How her breath would catch and her stomach contract as she remembered the hardness of his thighs through his jeans and his narrow waist under her

32

hands. And how, hearing the sound of his voice, deep and urging, and his suggestive laugh, she'd shiver, smile in her sleep, and wake up smiling.

But what did we do so special, Viyella wondered now as the mist curled her hair and tiny drops fell down the back of her neck, that filled those days with sunlight?

They had followed ancient cart roads through the back-woods, Jimmy kicking an old whiskey bottle as he sauntered along, his hands deep in his pockets as he whistled. Once they had passed the remains of a burned cabin—a heap of rubbish with a lonely, charred chimney. Whose? Viyella had wondered. What had happened? She had stopped, momentarily sad, not knowing why.

"Hey, Vi! C'mon!" Jimmy had tugged at her. "The water tower. Let's climb it!"

He was off, Viyella running after him. They raced, laughing, and Viyella leaned against the steel ladder, panting, even as Jimmy's clay-stained shoes worked their way up the rungs.

"Jimmy!" she called out to him. "Be careful." Oh, if he slipped, if he fell.

But he only laughed at her. "You should see things from here, Vi," he said, halfway up.

But she hung back, afraid. "Way off there," he pointed. His body moved dangerously on the ladder, and she shuddered. "I can see clear to Charlotte."

His voice grew fainter as he climbed, and finally at the top he paused, speechless. The wind played with his black hair, and she knew his eyes would be squinted against the light, peering into the distance, toward far-off things and wondrous sights over the tops of the pines. He looked so small up there, so far away. "Oh, Jimmy," Viyella sighed. All the things he was going to do!

"Going there someday," he told her when he came down. "Going to get out of here. Real soon."

"Leave home? Leave here for sure?"

"Sure am," he said confidently with a swagger. "See the state. See the world," he boasted. "Then I'll decide where I'll settle. *If* I settle."

Settle. The Kieffers never seemed to light anywhere very long, she thought. They were always moving on, looking for something here, there, and everywhere yonder; no one could tell what, and they hardly knew themselves. Shiftless, some folks said, her father Woodrow Redfern among them; no count. They'd pack up today and be off tomorrow, sometimes in such a hurry that they'd leave the water boiling on the stove, a log smoldering in the fireplace, or a sorry-looking chicken pecking among the leavings thrown out the back door. But they always came back again, sooner or later. Apt to, when winter set in.

They did. Didn't they? Viyella felt a pang of fear more sharp than when she had watched Jimmy climb to the top of the ladder with his shirttail waving in the breeze, a dread and sadness greater than when she had pondered on the forlorn remnants of the cabin and its life, long gone. But she smiled at him, encouraging. "What then, Jimmy?" she asked.

"No planting or plowing for me," he bragged. He socked a fist into his other hand. "No sir. Gonna go places, do things. No telling where I'll end up."

"Take me, Jimmy, take me," she pleaded, surprising herself. But Emerald would have climbed the water tower a step behind him, Viyella thought, ashamed of her fear.

"Maybe, Vi, maybe," he answered thoughtfully; she could almost see him turning it over in his mind. "But I might need someone to stay t'home, behind, you know? Never had much of a home," he said wistfully, almost longingly she thought, as if yearning for something he never had known and wasn't sure he wanted, something other people had and took for granted. "Might need someone to keep a place for me, somewheres." He frowned into the distant blue mountains and the uncertain future. Then, giving his head a quick shake, he tucked his shirt into his tight jeans, ready to move on. Viyella reached for his restless hand and held it tightly in her own.

There was a clearing behind Vinny's store, deep in the piney woods, and sometimes they had gone there. They had lain on the ground and propped their feet up on a stump to stare at the lazy clouds above. Or they had sat in the shade of a tall pine, leaning against its friendly bark, and gazed off across the fields into the blue smoke haze, smelling the pungent scent. They had watched the moving shadows on the sand, heard the murmuring branches overhead, and the slippery pine needles had tickled their skin.

And they had talked and talked.

But what did we ever find to say? Viyella wondered now. How was there so much?

And they had kissed.

"Don't be afraid, sweet darlin'. I won't hurt you. Won't hurt at all." Jimmy's voice was hoarse, but his hands were gentle, and Viyella couldn't bear to leave him, to drag herself away. She always had to go back and touch him again and again. And when he was gone, she had craved the feel of him. The sound of his voice was a living thing.

Oh, but that was back in the sandhills in the sunlit days so long ago, another time, another life.

Feelings. Where had they all gone? she asked herself early on this Sunday morning. What was there in their place? Not peace. Loss.

Fella began to howl, and there were rousing noises from the house. Viyella got up and went to Jimmy to inspect his wound. With the baby secure in one arm, she took his hand in the other and studied the bruised thumb.

"Sure is a sight," she sympathized. "That hammer always did have a slippery handle. Seems to want to jump right out its skin. Hmmm," she soothed, shifting Fella to the other shoulder. "Wait till I get a poultice. Won't take long."

When she returned, her fingers were tender and gentle on his.

five

BACK IN THE sandhills, Emerald had lived with her grandmother. Her mother had run off with a handsome Black Irishman, who wandered over the countryside doing odd jobs here and there. When she had tired of living on songs and promises, she'd skulked home in the dark of night, but no one saw her again.

Some said she'd run off as soon as she was strong enough, leaving behind the black-haired, green-eyed baby, the only reminder of Ryan McCullough. Others said she'd never set foot inside the door, just dropped the baby on the porch, knowing its whimpering would draw attention. People thought maybe the grandmother shooed her away the minute she saw her and took the baby for safekeeping. Whatever, she disappeared the way she had come, and Emerald was raised in the Carolina sandhills.

Emerald's grandmother was part Cherokee and was thought to be named Margaret Blueflower. She lived far out on the edge of the community, in a tiny shack that the Rockfish and Aberdeen, piled high with fresh-cut pine and flatcar loads of sand, shook as it chugged by.

All her life there Emerald lived with the sounds of trains in her ears: the warning blast in the noon heat, the lonesome cry at dusk. She often stood by the tracks as close as she dared, sometimes returning the engineer's friendly wave, more often motionless, solemnly watching the long line of cars wind out of sight through the tall pines. Later, when she had learned to read, she spelled out the names on their sides: Santa Fe, Erie Lackawanna, Louisville and Nashville, and whispered them to herself, sing-song. The music of faraway places: Seaboard, Delaware and Hudson, Nickel Plate Road.

People stood off from Margaret Blueflower, black and white alike a little afraid of her, but respectful. Or she stood off from them. She scratched out a living with chickens and hens and vegetables in her neat, bare yard. She made beautiful quilts of old rags to sell in town to visitors, sold roasted peanuts, and baked pecan cookies. She stood very straight, her gray hair clasped severely back at the nape of her neck, and her black eyes stared directly at you, giving nothing out, nothing away. She kept to herself, held her head proudly, and no one knew how old she was or what she had seen.

And neither did Emerald. Margaret Blueflower was a silent woman, going steadily about her tasks, speaking only to direct the girl to wash, to starch her dress, to build the fire, to hush her crying, to carry the fudge in to Mrs. Blaney.

When Emerald started school, she thought she'd burst with all the things she had on her mind: the sun, warm and gentle on her skin in early spring, the mourning dove calling out to her, Cannon Ball puffing by at noon. But she soon learned that school was a place where you were quiet too and didn't talk unless you raised your hand and were called on. And then the other children laughed because what she had to say had nothing to do with the words and pictures in books. She soon learned to be as tight-lipped as her grandmother.

At recess, when the children exploded into the school yard, shouting and running and dancing, she hung back and stayed aloof, until the day they ringed her round, taunting and jeering. She stood in the middle, her head high, and said nothing. Then she suddenly reached down, picked up a clod of dirt, and flung it at her tormentors. Surprised, they stood there a minute without moving while another clod hit and another. Then they closed in.

When she came home that day, her dress torn, her knees scraped, her hair tangled with mud, there were no tearstains on her dark cheeks. Margaret Blueflower nodded, her eyes fierce but her hands gentle, expert, as she washed her up. The next day Emerald was sent to the Colored School.

No one spoke to her here, either. The children backed off and looked at her from the corners of their eyes, nudging and whispering behind their hands. They were always giggling and punching each other and whooping it up. "Whoo-eee" they'd yell, rolling their eyes, she never knew at what. They stopped abruptly when she came by.

Ignored by the white and feared by the black, belonging neither one place nor the other, Emerald went silently each day to school and back, then to town and back, toting her grandmother's wares. Even when the women smiled as she delivered pies and cakes and they paid her, sometimes handing her a piece of ribbon for her hair or a penny for herself, she never curtsied and said "Thank you, ma'am" but only stared with her great dark eyes and made them uncomfortable. Soon they never reached to pat her on the head, never said "Well, now, how pretty we are today" or "How good it smells. Your Gran bakes the best in the county" or "Sews the best in all Carolina." And soon there were no more pretties, either.

So more and more often Emerald stood by the railroad track, singing her songs in her low-key, tuneless voice: Chesapeake and Ohio, Milwaukee Road.

Overnight Emerald's dresses were too small; they stretched tight across her shoulder blades, ripping Margaret's carefully sewn seams under the armpits. Abruptly she was sent back to the white school, the Junior High over in Gassetts.

Overnight, too, she discovered something. Older boys looked at her from under lowered lids and took to grinning slyly when they thought her head was bent over her books. Soon a group of them were hanging around after school, talking, laughing, looking at her knowingly, and shoving each other to sit behind her on the school bus.

The girls didn't bother with her, but it wasn't long before Emerald learned to copy them. She saw she didn't have to say much, just act a little bit: "Ooooh, Billy!" with a small curving smile and her wide-eyed stare, or "Hey, Tom Joe, you stop that!" with a high voice and a sharp little giggle. She walked with her shoulders straight back, not rounded by school books, and the boys watched and nudged each other.

Jimmy Kieffer was the boldest. He sometimes whispered in her ear, and though she looked at him blankly, he touched her and gave a soft whistle. After she met him in the woods behind Vinny's store, he brought her a shiny glittering pin from the five and ten. She hid it in a Quaker Oats box, pushed way under the far side of her bed. Soon the box was almost full of trinkets: a satiny pink bow, a sparkling bracelet of blue cut stones, a gold ring too small to wear but pretty to hold and turn over in her palm. In the early morning when the sun was just coming up, she'd take out her treasures, spread them on her bed for the light to catch, and run them through her fingers.

Then, one day, without a sound, Margaret Blueflower walked in and watched her from the doorway. Still not speaking, she strode swiftly to the bed, gathered the trinkets into her apron, and slapped hard with a stiff, rigid hand across Emerald's cheek. The force of the blow brought unexpected, unused tears to Emerald's eyes, but her lips pressed as close together as her grandmother's. And then there were no more trinkets.

Soon after, Margaret Blueflower began to age. There was nothing any different to be seen, really; only she grew thinner, the hollows in her cheeks deepening until her face seemed etched in sharp stone, and her step slowed. Her back was as straight as ever, her head as high, but when she couldn't catch a ride with Vinny, she began to use Charley's taxi to take her goods to town.

Emerald watched Viyella Redfern constantly. Viyella was different. She couldn't laugh and giggle as Emerald had learned to do, and she had no silly things to say either, but there was something about her. Jimmy Kieffer was always going up to her, even though Viyella turned away, and showing off in the school yard if she was around, calling too loud to the other boys.

And folks said that Viyella could sing, that her voice in the choir at Centertown Church could be heard through all the others, deep and harmonious, blending over and under, weaving them all together. She sang in the Christmas Pageant Jimmy's last year at school. Dressed in blue, flowing robes, she bent over a cradle on the stage, her hands outstretched. Her golden hair made a halo around her face, and people said she looked like an angel. Jimmy never took his eyes from her, and Emerald never took hers from Jimmy. What did *he* care for singing? He didn't care much for anything except sporting around with the boys and one other thing Emerald knew of. What was it about Viyella?

The answer came when Viyella left school and married him. Emerald laughed with the other girls and poked fun at Viyella. "Ha! She got him! She trapped Jimmy Kieffer! Who'd 'a thought it! Won't trap him long, though. Not him!"

Emerald waited, but as the months went by, she was disappointed to see that she had been fooled just like the others. Then before too long, Jimmy went off to Fayetteville to find a job, leaving Viyella behind.

It was a big car from the North, long and black and arrogant, that pulled out of the space in front of the Exchange. Charley, heading down the street in his old taxi, was hit before he could turn. The old taxi spun, its wheels skidding in the sand, and crashed into the pine by the side of the road. Margaret Blueflower was sitting in the front, and her pecan pie, held carefully in her lap, was mashed and splattered beyond repair. And so was she.

Emerald buried her on a Monday and packed such things as she wanted before she closed the house. In the bottom of a chest, under Margaret's worn old gray cardigan, was the Quaker Oats box full of trinkets. Emerald fondled each one a long time, dreaming. Then she took them outside and laid them on the railroad track for Cannonball to smash.

She watched the train come by at noon: Great Northern, Union Pacific, the Soo Line, heading south to Fayetteville. As the last car vanished around the bend into the piney woods, she waved it out of sight, then carefully picked her way along the railroad ties. She could feel the gravel through the thin soles of her shoes, and her heel caught on splintered wood.

She'd catch a ride by Aberdeen and go in search of Jimmy Kieffer.

six

H. A. HAD BEEN only a few months old when Jimmy decided to try his luck in Fayetteville. He was tired of working in the fields and sick of sitting down at the table with Woodrow Redfern. Then too, Bessa, his mother-in-law, was always around, bossing him, saying "Eat this, Jimmy, eat that, Jimmy; try the

41

turnips. A married man needs to keep up his strength," with a wink and a raucous laugh. And Viyella, busy with her baby, only smiled at him, a deep blush staining her cheeks.

He was gone a long while, and when he came home, he was cocky and swaggering, full of himself. He tipped back in his chair, blowing cigar smoke over the food as he treated them to tales of the city. But Bessa soon put a stop to that. "You blow that smoke outdoors, you hear? None of that in my kitchen, Jimmy Kieffer!" And soon he was back in the fields.

Often in the evenings, when the sun went down, Woodrow got out his banjo. Sometimes just he and Viyella would sing, he doing his part:

> *We are a band of brothers*
> *And native to the soil*

and then she doing hers:

> *My homespun dress is plain I know*
> *My hat's palmetto too*
> *But then it shows what Southern girls*
> *For Southern rights will do.*

Other times, Woodrow sang his stories alone:

> *'Tis old Stonewall the rebel that leans on his sword*
> *And while we are waiting, prays low to the Lord*
> *Now each Cavalier who loves honor and right*
> *Let him follow the feather of Stuart tonight.*

They sang love songs, too, Viyella softly sad, her eyes staring at the flames, the fragrance of the hickory smoke adding its own poignance to the sorrowful words and her haunting voice. She was far away, her face dreaming in the

42

light from the fire, a stranger to Jimmy. He wanted her then, wanted to know her, but she eluded him.

The firelight softened her sharp features; the shadows made the hollows of her face mysterious. She stared, lost to him, until he called her back and took her to bed. And even then, with the moonlight streaking her bright hair, her eyes often focused beyond him on something he couldn't see, and her head turned as if listening to voices he couldn't hear, until he brought her back.

"Hey, Vi, Sugar." He poked her playfully. "How'dja like that? Hey? More?"

Then she'd look at him and touch his cheek and sometimes kiss the cleft between his neck and shoulder.

"Jimmy," she'd whisper, but he fretted and wondered and grew restless.

Often they'd all sing together one of Charley's songs:

> *O he nebber count de bubbles*
> *While dere's water in de Spring*
> *De feller hab no troubles*
> *While he got dis song to sing!*

And off they would go, feet tapping, hands clapping, rollicking along, all joining in, even Bessa. Only Jimmy fidgeted and was silent.

Then he would see Viyella's eyes sparkle, her face lit up by more than firelight. There was laughter in her lilting voice, but it was separate from him; Jimmy was an outsider. What was so funny about "The Blue Tail Fly" or "Goober Peas"? But Woodrow would laugh too and slap his knee with his big hand. Together, with scarcely a nod between them, they could hit a note at the same time in harmony, and when, the song ended, Viyella turned to him breathless, her cheeks flushed, her laughter outright now along with Woodrow's guffaw, Jimmy sulked. What was making her so gay? So

43

joyful? Wasn't him. He couldn't sing a tune and keep it steady, not a one. Couldn't see the fun in it either.

Who was Viyella, his wife? Jimmy sometimes asked himself. What was she thinking on; what pleasured her so? Her eyes didn't shine as much for him, her pretty mouth smiling. Viyella laughing! She who was usually so serious.

It came from minding her brothers and sisters too young, he thought, from taking the worries off her Mama while Bessa whistled and sauntered off to the fields with the men. Or from being by herself so much, way out on the farm, with no one to talk to, chatter at, except young'uns who didn't understand, or the cardinals pecking after the sunflower seed she had set out, or the wind sighing in the chimney when the cold came. She took on too much, worked too hard too young, alone all day until her Mama, and especially her Daddy, came home to cheer her at dusk. And then her heart would liven.

But she didn't really need the cheering like other people did, Jimmy thought: the sly story, the poke in the ribs to make her chuckle, or even the company of the folks at Vinny's or in the church vestibule when Preacher got done on a Sunday. That was the mystery he couldn't fathom.

Viyella smiled over the soft rain soothing her cheeks in April, holding her face up to catch it, her eyelashes damp and spikey, stuck together, giving her a wondering look. Or laughed, skipping along the sandy road for no reason but that the sun was warm on her back, making her long hair golden. She was happy to see the first pussy willow come at the end of winter and excited when she watched the cotton clouds building up to a storm in summer. She felt it in the air, smelled it, the change freshening her skin.

And the joy the child brought her! Jimmy shook his head, mystified. She made a game of him. Sometimes she blew a fly off the baby's nose, puff! and giggled like little girls in a school yard covering their mouths with their hands, their

44

heads together. She tickled H. A. with an old straw under the chin, as he, Jimmy might, for lack of something else to do, but then she turned it on herself, smiling so sweet, and the baby chortled. She danced with H. A. too, holding him tight in her arms, high-stepping to a tune of her own making. She made soldiers out of sticks and marched them up to him, plop into his little belly, and both fell back with laughter; Woodrow too, if he was around. Carrying on.

She even seemed to enjoy her sorrowing, her tears always coming. Damndest woman for weeping, Jimmy thought, over the robins drunk on the berries in December, their puffed little bodies dazed and reeling, then squashed on the highway; the daffodils beaten with hail; Cannonball going on through at twilight. She pondered on the land changing color, darkening at nightfall, and the whippoorwill calling to her. What was in her head? Her heart? Jimmy knew it was no use to tell him; it made no sense when she tried to. But he craved her secret.

The trouble was, he craved Emerald too. Emerald never ailed or turned in on herself birthing babies. She was always ready for whatever he wanted to do, to laugh at his jokes, too.

And he got lonesome; he needed company. There was another little gal down to Fayetteville who had caught his fancy before Emerald got there—Bonnie Dee, wiggling her bottom at him as she fetched his beer at the A-1 Cafe. You wouldn't catch her worrying alone over blue jays and cardinals, sundown over the fields, and a child's cry, thought Jimmy. Nor Emerald. Emerald and Bonnie Dee didn't confuse and baffle a man beyond his wits, didn't mix up his feelings. They took care of a man, and they didn't ask bothersome questions, didn't leave him with any either.

But Viyella comforted him that way too, giving, not holding back, never, and why was that, with all her no's beforehand? He could study on it all his days and never know. But

45

then she left a man mixed up, his feelings nagging at him. Even though there was something she gave, there was something he missed, but it was surely there for him to reach and take. If he could get hold of it.

Who knew what Viyella was thinking on? Be damned if he could understand her.

She wasn't even twenty yet, he thought, but there were no trinkets or pretty clothes for Viyella, no picnics or parties. She was alone again, but it wasn't the lap child her Mama used to leave behind for her to mind that she tended and crooned to; it was her own, his. And the happiness glowed on her as she rocked it in her arms, like the way the light of the full moon shone as they lay in their iron bed. Joy in the morning, sweet yearning at dusk. Who knew Viyella? What was it she wanted? Where? What did she have he didn't?

Distant places didn't matter to her, he knew, cities and lights, buildings higher than the oak back of Centertown Church, folks hurrying by, but always near enough to josh with and smack up a beer. There were wondrous sights to see, but Viyella took pleasure from a coffee cup steaming up the window on a frosty day, from drawing pictures in the cloudiness for H. A. It was enough for her.

No, that didn't explain it all. Jimmy frowned. There was something else too. Just seeing the line of mountains far off, she told him. She didn't know where or who she was if she couldn't see the mountains. She needed them, and the long-leaf pine, and the sand between her toes as she walked barefoot in the yard, and the smell of her Mama's hickory logs burning in first autumn. A fire's a fire, thought Jimmy, but no, there was more meaning to it than that, said Viyella.

Jimmy craved her secret. What was it she had and he didn't? The warmth on the old brick hearth and Woodrow's love? A child's fist tight around her fingers? Her Mama's kitchen, the sounds of pots and pans, chicken cooking to make the mouth water? Jimmy liked his vittles, his fire, his

46

baby; he was proud that H. A. was healthy and sound. But it was more than this for Viyella. It was some other thing. Deeper. And what need had he, Jimmy Kieffer, of the other?

But when he came back from Fayetteville, there was a sadness on her, heavier than before, more mystifying than her pondering.

seven

WHEN JIMMY left, Viyella knew that Emerald had gone too. You couldn't hide anything in a community as small as this one. Even though she stayed at home most of the time with her baby, still, when she went to Vinny's store for Mama to pick up salt and flour and sugar, she didn't see Emerald strutting around. And at church, there were the women. She could hear their smothered whispers when she came near, feel their shaming looks on her, their pitying, amused glances. They talked down to her, snickering inside, as if they knew something she didn't. And when Jimmy finally came home from Fayetteville, there were all kinds of signs that everything was different.

Was this how you guessed that your husband was untrue? How did you know for sure? You could tell by the little ways and tricks that gave him away: the two tickets to the amusement park at Morehead City that fell out of his pocket; the strong fragrance of White Lilac saturating his checkered handkerchief; the way he sometimes stared into space, then asked "What?" vaguely, yet abruptly, as if jerked out of a dream when she spoke to him. What did he brood on, staring off like that? she wondered. What did he see? *Whom* did he see?

It was that he no longer really looked at her, saw *her*, Viyella, or quite met her eyes. And Emerald had left so suddenly after he had.

It was all these things, and a strangeness to his touch, a holding back, as if his mind and heart weren't there at all.

Whatever it was, sometimes Viyella found she couldn't catch her breath. Her heart pounded violently in sudden fear and senseless panic. She looked at him as if he were someone she hadn't seen before, not Jimmy Kieffer, her husband. Nothing would ever be the same again. Ever.

Viyella knew.

eight

ONE NIGHT Woodrow was pensive. Bessa had been sharp all day, snapping at them all, sharp even with the baby H. A. "Got a crick in my side," she apologized, "biting at me." But the next minute she told Viyella to get out of her kitchen, she could sure do up the dishes herself. And then she demanded to know why Jimmy didn't put his time to good use and fix that loose post on the porch? And for that matter, why didn't Woodrow make himself of some account?

Out came the banjo, thumpety thump, to drown her out. And then Woodrow slowed his notes, his fingers lingering on the strings, creating a strange, mournful sound.

Black, black, black is the color of my true love's hair

Jimmy stopped his wiggling and sat perfectly still. Viyella felt his quiet, and glancing away from the fire, she turned to look at him. He didn't see her.

48

If she on earth no more I'd see
My life would quickly fade away

"Stop!" Viyella cried, hardly knowing what she did. "Don't sing that any more!"

Black, black, black . . .

Surprised, Woodrow's fingers slackened to a few harmless chords, and Viyella, having clapped her hands to her ears, now dropped them sheepishly in her lap.

"I . . . I'm sorry," she mumbled, looking away from her father's steady gaze. "I guess . . ."

"What's troubling you, Vi?" he asked gently.

"Smoke stung my eyes, is all," she answered, though the flames were shooting straight up the chimney.

"Well, let's sing something more sprightly!" Woodrow's tempo quickened. " 'Go tell Aunt Rhody.' C'mon, sing Vi."

But she couldn't. And Jimmy sat in his own world, never noticing.

The next day Viyella was listless, scarcely rocking the baby held limply in her arms. Her crooning was a moaning without a tune, without comfort.

Woodrow found her thus on his way to the fields.

"Bright morning, Vi. Look yonder! The cardinal."

She rocked in silence, her head bowed.

"No time to rock now, Vi. No lullabies right after breakfast. Work to do. Come along with me, such a day!"

"Baby's fretting," she answered without looking up.

"Well, now, Vi, sometimes they must fret. You know that, and H. A.'s about getting too big to be held."

"He can't settle to nothing," she went on, as if she hadn't heard him. "Chewing on my finger don't help, nor sugar water. Nothing."

Woodrow looked at the golden top of her head, her hair

49

falling gently over her face, and at H. A.'s little hand gripping his mother's arm.

"Damn shiftless, rootless Kieffers!" he exploded so angrily it seemed to shake him where he stood, down to his grass-stained boots.

"Papa!" Viyella's head jerked back, the fine hair sweeping over her shoulder.

"Jimmy!" Woodrow bellowed. "Where the hell are you? Beat the stuffing out of him, damn ignorant womanizer!"

"Papa!"

"Jimmy! Get moving on down here!" Woodrow shouted and smacked a fist into his flattened palm.

"Please, Papa," Viyella begged, her eyes filling with tears. "Don't say nothing. He's leaving soon again anyways."

"Hell he is." With a few long steps, Woodrow crossed to her. He bent down awkwardly, his arms enfolding her and the baby, and pressed her face close to his rough plaid jacket.

"Aw, Vi," he said, his words smothered against her soft cheek. "Poor little Vi."

It was too much; she leaned against him weeping, her shoulders heaving with sobs coming up from her shoes, her heart, her whole being.

"Hush, now hush." He held her until he heard Jimmy's whistle, the creak of the bedsprings as he got out of bed, the stomp of his feet on the floor.

"Vi." Woodrow pushed her gently away, one hand still firmly holding her, the other raising her chin. "Stand tall, Vi," he said as he lifted her. "Hold yourself proud."

Her eyes were glistening, her collar damp, but she smiled at Jimmy when he came in.

"Hey? What's going on? Vi?"

"Baby's fussing."

"Set him down and let's have some grits. I'm real hungry."

"You're late, too," Woodrow said grimly, his fist clenched at his side.

50

Jimmy didn't seem to hear. "C'mon, Vi." He began to whistle again. "Hustle along."

He gave her a tap to push her on her way, and Woodrow's firm arm dropped. Hold yourself proud, Vi.

"You crying again?" Jimmy asked, exasperated. "God damn, what over this time?"

"A cardinal, Jimmy. Saw it out the window."

"A cardinal!" Jimmy snorted. But she could see he was in high good humor this morning. It was a blue and golden day, and she knew his feet were itching to be off again.

He shrugged his shoulders good-naturedly and grinned at his father-in-law.

"Never will understand women." He chuckled. "You, Woodrow?"

Woodrow clamped his teeth, his jaw working, and his fist opened and closed at his side.

"Eh?" Jimmy gave an exaggerated sigh, as if the whole world in general, and women in particular, baffled him, were beyond him, but he'd be a good fella about it; he didn't care, no skin off his nose. Sun was out!

With the baby cradled in her arm, Viyella went to the kitchen to get his breakfast. Jimmy followed, whistling.

He stayed until Jenny Sue was born six months later; then off he went again, to Winston-Salem this time, High Point, Warsaw. What was there in Warsaw for Jimmy Kieffer to do?

Bessa was beginning to ail. Her stomach ached from time to time, and when she set off for the fields in the morning, she was sometimes bent double. And more and more often she quit at noon, stretching out on the bed.

"I don't know, Woodrow, I don't know," she'd mumble, her eyes searching the whitewashed ceiling, the rough beams overhead, for some answer, then fearfully meeting his eyes when he sat down beside her. Viyella brought warm cloths to lay on her belly, and the next day or the day after she'd be up again. Soon it was always the day after, and then the day after that. So when Jimmy at last came home again a year later, they were glad to see him. Woodrow needed a hand, and Bessa, silent and musing, was fading before their eyes.

But Jimmy didn't stay long. Woodrow had taken to playing his banjo more and more, and the rasping noise of its missing strings and Woodrow's harsh voice grated on Jimmy's nerves. He had heard of good jobs at the Marine Base, he said, east, nearly on the coast.

"Don't go, Jimmy, please," Viyella pleaded. "Stay on and help Papa with the crops."

"I told you before, honey, I can't be no farmer. Not me."

He paced restlessly around their small room. "No sir! I'm going places!" Then, looking at her all huddled up and woebegone, he sank down beside her on the iron bed. "Sugar, I'll send for you, soon's I can." He smoothed her golden hair. "I'll come fetch you before you have time to miss me. Don't fret so, sweetheart. Give us a kiss."

So he went on ahead. He was gone so many months this time that Viyella wondered if he would ever be back, or if the rest of her life would be spent nursing her mother, tending her children, and watching her father in his futile struggle to battle alone the underbrush and weeds that stifled his once fertile fields.

nine

WHEN H. A. was four and old enough to help, Viyella often sent him, if she didn't need him at home, along with Papa. Then Woodrow whistled and loped along in his old jaunty fashion, and Viyella watched the boy trying to copy him, his small shoulders swaying from side to side, until the high grass hid all but the top of his bright head.

Papa always stopped at the corner of the old south plot. Here where the land rose slightly and, far off like smoke, lay the distant blue of the hills, he leaned on a post of the split-rail fence, hoisted H. A. up on the bars so he could see too, and paused a moment to survey his farm.

"Never ceases to pleasure me." He sighed. "Look yonder, H. A. Them's the Blue Ridge Mountains way off there."

The boy followed the pointing finger, squinting his eyes against the sun just as Woodrow did.

"And there, look there, H. A. Cotton's so high. Fields is so green." He sighed again, content, and when there was time, the work all done or not much left to do, he pulled out his pipe and lit up.

"Won't hurt your Gramma none out here." He chuckled. For a while he puffed in silence, checking all four corners of his farm and the woods beyond, making sure all was in order.

"It's a world of its own, our own," he said. "Someday it'll be yours, H. A., to work on and tend. Like that?"

"Yes, sir," H. A. answered soberly.

Woodrow tousled H. A.'s hair and raised himself up beside him on the rail.

"Used to be redskins in them woods. Cherokee." Woodrow's voice dropped, and a pleasurable shiver crept up H. A.'s spine. Now the cabin seemed far off and lonely over the fields, and the woods looked dark and menacing with all kinds of creatures living and creeping within. If he held his breath, he was sure he could hear the soft beat of a tom-tom and stealthy footsteps coming closer and closer. Once when a covey of quail flew up with a sudden noise, he jumped and nearly fell. Woodrow's large arm reached around his shoulders and held him protectively. "Folks say Miss Margaret Blueflower was an Indian. Did you know that? She must have had some tales to tell!"

Woodrow had plenty himself. He scared H. A. with stories of raids and captives, happily seeing the brown eyes grow large with excitement.

He'd go on to hunts he and Vinny'd been on, the painter he'd shot, the fish he'd caught. Then his face and voice would grow solemn, and he'd launch into the War.

"Bravest men of all, our Tar Heels. Don't you ever forget it, H. A. First at Bethel, farthest at Gettysburg, and last at Appomattox."

"Yes, sir," answered H. A., serious.

"Know why we're called Tar Heels? Had a lot of pitch and such round these parts, and everyone knew it. Well, back in the War, in a fierce bad battle, everyone ran, I'm sorry to relate, except the Carolina boys. They held their ground and fought. Sometime after, they met that regiment that turned tail. Would you reckon, H. A., those yellow fellas would poke fun at us?"

"At *us*?"

"Yup. Jeered, they did, laughing, probably just ashamed, but they hooted, 'Any more tar down in the Old North State?' 'Not a bit,' we says. 'Old Jeff's bought it up.' That was Jefferson Davis, the President of the Confederacy, son. 'What's he going to do with it?' they asks. 'He's going to put it on your heels to make you stick better in the next fight!' Heh, heh. So ever since then we're Tar Heels. Not a bad thing to be, H. A."

"No, sir." He grinned proudly back at his Grandpa, holding himself straight, chest out.

"There was a boy, not so much older than you, sad to relate," Woodrow started again reflectively. "He fell at Shiloh. Found a picture . . ."

54

But by this time, H. A.'s head had dropped against his grandfather's plaid sleeve and he was fast asleep. Woodrow carried him home, the weight precious in his arms. When they reached the doorstep, he set H. A. down and they took one last look at the fields in the twilight.

"See all the different colors, H. A. Reds and browns and yellows and greens and blues. Seems like the Lord was in a gay mood when he made this land. Then the sun goes down and it's like He had a lot on His mind. A brooding country. A deep place."

It was getting on toward lowering dark now, time to go in by the fire. Woodrow paused a moment longer.

"Always meant to set out some peach trees, off there in the corner. Good living from them if there's any luck, and what a sight to behold come spring!"

He opened the door. "Too late now, too late. Maybe you'll do it, boy."

ten

SLOWLY MAMA worsened, and as Viyella grew large again she needed H. A. at home to mind Jenny Sue, while she fetched water and sassafrass root and sang hymns to her mother, or bright sassy songs, as Mama's mood dictated.

"It's the Lord's will, Vi, I know that," Mama groaned, tossing and turning, never at peace. "But what is He studying on? Why does it take so long for some?" she sighed. "And too quick for others?"

"Hush, Mama," Viyella soothed. "You'll be well and strong again."

55

"You ain't fooling me none."

Was that thin, sighing voice Mama's? Viyella hardly recognized it.

"No, ma'am."

Mama reached to grab Viyella's hand, clinging tightly. "You've always pleasured me, Viyella. I should have told you before this. Reckon mothers take their daughters for granted. And all of a sudden, it's too late. You remember that, Vi. I . . ." Then as a spasm shook her, she choked, and the words were lost in her sobs. "Daughter, why? What is it He has in His heart?"

Next time, months later, when Jimmy came home, he drove up in a shiny blue car, blasting the horn all the way from Vinny's store, it seemed; they heard him soon enough. It was a big, ugly-looking thing, a '37 Packard, but Jimmy couldn't stop walking around it, touching the fender, pounding the hood, and loudly praising its virtues to anyone who would listen. He was more excited, more proud of it than he was of his tiny new daughter Elizabeth Ann, black-haired and blue-eyed like himself, lying quiet in the cradle in the kitchen.

"Aw, she's always asleep," he protested. "Sure, she's pretty, but look, Woodrow, you seen this?" He pointed to the hubcaps proudly.

Jimmy said it was true there were good jobs at the Marine Base, and good pay. He had gone to see about one while he was away, and now he had a house there for them, too. It needed fixing, but he would do that. It had a roof and was built high off the ground; there was even a good garden space for Viyella. And he was anxious to be off.

But Viyella was loath to leave her mother and for weeks thought of one reason after another to stay. "How would Mama and Papa manage?" she asked. "Give Papa a hand until the crops are in and he can tend Mama," she begged. Wait until she had her own strength back. Her milk would dry and spoil on the long trip. Wait until Elizabeth Ann was older.

"The hell with it!" Jimmy finally yelled and slammed out the door. The car started up in a roar, the racket startling a flock of birds nesting in the blackberry bushes by the side of the road.

Mama's eyes pleaded and were enough to hold Viyella back. This was her mother, this poor puny little woman, who once had stridden vigorously off to the fields with the men, whistling as loud as they, hardly looking back or waving to the row of little ones lined up on the porch, left in Viyella's care.

But Woodrow said, "Go on, Vi. He needs you; rightly so. And there's nothing more to do here except wait. Wait," he repeated softly. And to be ready for Jimmy's return, he dismantled the iron bed for them to take along.

They tied the mattress on the roof of the car, secured the bedstead on top of it, and heaped their few belongings on the back seat. Viyella held Elizabeth Ann in her arms, and Jenny Sue sat beside her on H. A.'s lap, her head across her mother's stomach. At the last minute, Mama, wrapped in a heavy shawl pulled tight around her scrawny shoulders, wisps of hair poking out from under her bonnet, teetered out to the yard and shoved her old prized copper teakettle through the window.

"Here, take it. Do," she said as Viyella protested. "I won't be needing it." Then she crept back up the steps and, leaning against Woodrow, waved them out of sight.

And Viyella wept, not because she was leaving, but because the mother she knew had already gone.

She mourned all the way, in spite of Jimmy's promises and chatter. But then she felt the quickening of life under the weight of Jenny Sue's head, Elizabeth Ann cooed in her sleep, and the touch of H. A.'s staunch shoulder next to hers was warm and filled her with a certain peace.

They came to this flat land here, the low country in the east, to the house off the highway, beyond the Bloody Bucket. The first thing Viyella did was fill the copper kettle with greens. Then she swept the grimy kitchen clean and pinned the Western Auto calendar on the wall. She tacked burlap, dyed in berries, deep blue, up at the window. Whenever the greens withered, she replaced them with flowers in season: holly, redbud, honeysuckle, and she polished the copper kettle over and over again until it gleamed and shone. But whatever she did, this place would never be home. Never.

part two

*In Rama was there a voice heard, lamentation,
and weeping, and great mourning, Rachel weeping
for her children, and would not be comforted,
because they are not.*

MATTHEW 2:18

MOSTLY VIYELLA
dreamed of the sandhills in the evening. After supper, with
the children quiet and Jimmy sitting on the orange crate
puffing his cigar, her hands would lag in the dishwater, sometimes scraping the same pot over and over again, while her
eyes roamed out the window over the sink. It was that dusky
time when the birds were still and no wind stirred the
branches of the trees. But here the pines formed a black wall
against the darkening sky, a barrier she couldn't see beyond.
Their tall, straight trunks were bars, imprisoning her.

What was it she was dreaming of over the years? Her
Mama was gone, and her Papa had been put in the County
Home, wandering in his mind. They said he giggled like a
naughty little boy one minute, then pouted, his lip jutting
out, the next, spilled gravy down his shirt, and dropped his
spoon for someone else to pick up. Viyella sighed. The farm
must surely have gone all weedy now, tangled growth choking the rich fields, forsythia scraggling over the front win-
dows of the house, the chimney tumbling piece by piece with
each new rain that fell.

So what was it? Viyella wondered. The pungent smell of
Mama's wood fire on an autumn day, reaching out to her as
she walked home from school so long ago? There was woodsmoke here, too. Sometimes it hung in a gentle blue haze,
far off, softening the woods, and she stopped to breathe it
in, feeling again the school bag of books slap against her
skirt, the coldness of her cheeks, and the welcoming warmth
when she came inside. But nothing seemed as sharp or clear
or inviting as it had then, back in the sandhills.

Maybe it was that at home, where Route 101 crossed
Muleback right by Vinny's store, she could see the mountains. It's funny, Viyella thought now, how you never knew

you were climbing, but when you got there, the land fell away below the clearing, and far off, over the waves of green, were lines and lines of blue, dark, then lighter and lighter, fading off into the sky. She never had wanted to go to them, but she liked to look at them and needed to know they were there.

She remembered how they had been different colors at different times of the day and in different weathers: sometimes in a storm, nearly black; and in a light rain, a faint gray, almost invisible. But nearly always they were blue, the sky big above them. And how, seeing them, looking off from Vinny's porch, she hadn't felt closed in, but free and at peace at the same time.

Viyella's eyes strained through her dark window. She set the pot aside and twirled a cup around in the water.

> *Every night, when the sun goes in*
> *Every night, when the sun goes in*
> *Every night, when the sun goes in*
> *I hang my head, and lonesome cry.*

She sang softly, her voice like the wisp of woodsmoke, like the smell of it promising something, fading off, lost. If she could just find it, grasp it, hold on to it . . .

> *Pray the Lord, my train will come*
> *Pray the Lord, my train will come*
> *Pray the Lord, my train will come*
> *And carry me back, where I come from.*

But what was there? What was she dreaming of? What was it?

"Hey, old gal, ain't you done yet?" Jimmy asked, the

orange crate creaking as he got up. "Them kids is restless; time for bed."

Now her eyes came back to the pan, the cup, her red hands stirring the water. Briskly she dumped the pan outside, spattering the hard-packed dirt by Jimmy's feet.

"H. A., c'mon. Time to come in," she called and then busied herself scrubbing faces, unbuttoning, tying up, brushing, tickling.

When they were all settled, she paused a moment by the kitchen window and looked out. It was all dark now, but still there stood the pines, guarding, blacker than the sky.

"Why are you so sad, Ma? What are you thinking about?"

"Nothing much, H. A. Grandma and Grampa and the mountains is all." She smiled at him. "And the woodsmoke in November."

Where was it? What was it? Something she had lost and couldn't find? Something she had never had and yearned for?

two

EVEN THOUGH the dog days hung on, more summer than fall, it was time to get ready for school. Viyella sat late into the night with her needle and thread, but there was little she could do about H. A.'s clothes. Let down as far as they would go, his jeans reached a point several inches above his bony ankle. There was no use, either, to drop pants of Jimmy's; H. A. was nearly as tall as his father, and even with an old laundry rope pulled tight and knotted securely, they bagged around him.

63

There was no telling where his waist left off and his skinny hips began. It was off to the Economy for him.

"Waste of good money," Jimmy grumbled. "No use spending any on him. He'll just shoot right out of everything before Christmas. You wait and see."

"He can't go to school like that," Viyella said. "All his bones sticking out in the cold and kids laughing at him. What if the rope was to come untied, then what? Like to die of shame. How would you feel about *that* story getting round? Shem Baker and them'd hoot you out of town." She unwound more thread from a spool, and catching it between her teeth, bit it firmly in two. "Besides, I can pass H. A.'s along to Thomas," she added logically, "and to Jee Paw too, he's getting so big. Anyways, there's shoes to get."

"Shoes!" Jimmy was outraged. "Just got him shoes last year." He glanced over to where H. A. stood and then looked down at his feet. They were undeniable. Tanned, tough, clay-stained, they extended from the wall almost to the rockers of Viyella's chair. " 'Least that's one worry I won't have about *him*." Jimmy jerked his thumb roughly in Fella's direction and stomped out, beckoning H. A. to follow him. Viyella bowed her head quickly to hide her tears until they were safely out the door and on their way to the store. Then she bent down and took Fella in her arms.

"Ma, this don't look good." Jenny Sue came in to model the bright red dress that only last year had been her most prized possession. "See? It's all washed out," she complained, "from when you hung it out in the sun."

Viyella put Fella down and surveyed her daughter from all angles. "Shouldn't have faded. *Blues* fade. Wonder what cheap dye they used in that. Pretty shade of pink, though."

"Oh, Ma, it looks terrible!" Jenny Sue wailed. "I can't go to school in *this*. Everybody will joke at me, and it's too tight. See?" She stretched back her arms and Viyella saw.

64

Jenny Sue was changing too. Somehow over the summer Viyella had missed seeing it; it was as gradual and slow as the grass growing so there was no one time you might say it was taller than yesterday; but in the autumn, there it was, two feet high, no longer the rough little stubble under foot, and you wondered how it got so tall. And when. Viyella sighed for the passing of the years and for her daughter and what lay ahead.

"Ain't it?" Jenny Sue cried eagerly. She placed a hand on her hip, cocked her head on one side, and smiled slyly up at her mother in the manner usually saved for Jimmy and the other men. But the batting, dark lashes over the coy, blue eyes were too much.

"I can make it a different color. Green would be right nice," Viyella said, studying the dress. "Would take, too. You can wear it a while yet, and it can be let out."

"Oh, Ma." Jenny Sue turned her mouth down crossly, looking in that second so incongruously like Jimmy denied that Viyella laughed aloud. But when she fingered the seams along the side to figure how much there was, she touched her daughter's body gingerly, avoiding the little bumps protruding so proudly and bravely under the material.

"Don't you fret none, darlin'," she said. The sadness, the foreboding, enveloped her like a heavy blanket, muffling her voice. "I'll make it nice," she promised, praying she could.

But they didn't have to worry. When Jimmy came in, H. A. shuffled in behind him, awkward in his new clothes, somehow as ill-fitting as the old ones, his bright, shiny new shoes looking as though they pained him every step. Jimmy carried a big white box under one arm.

Jenny Sue threw her mother a quick look of triumph and then flew at the box, all fingers, untying it as fast as she could.

"Hey, now," laughed Jimmy, "easy, sweetheart." He

kissed the back of her head bent over the package and played for a minute with the silky, blonde hair. "Got to be the prettiest gal in all of Onslow County!"

They all watched as Jenny Sue, her pale cheeks flushed with excitement, breathlessly pulled out the dress. All Viyella saw was fluttering yellow, but her heart sank. Jimmy had missed the grasses growing too. It was a little girl's pattern, lacy and puckered, no more suitable for Jenny Sue than a baby bonnet. In the silence, waiting with dread for Jenny Sue's scorn, Viyella suffered for Jimmy, who sat there leaning forward happily in anticipation of love and appreciation. Then, as he grew anxious, the smile slowly faded from his face, the light in his eyes flickered out in doubt.

"Looks real pretty," H. A. tried. It was one of those times his voice betrayed him, as out of control as his gangling hands and poorly housed feet encased in their stiff leather. "Prett" was low, the bull frog, but "tee" was the screech of the hoot owl. Torn between tears and laughter, Viyella choked on her words of praise.

Jimmy turned to stare in disbelief at his son, whose face was now reddening at an alarming rate, and didn't see his daughter holding the dress at arm's length, her nose wrinkled in distaste. When he turned back, her face was smooth, and her lips curved up sweetly in a smile.

"Thank you so much, Daddy," she said in a prissy little voice. "It's just beautiful."

Jimmy's face relaxed. "Come give your Daddy a kiss then, sugar." He held out his arms.

She went to him sedately, her lips and eyelashes brushing his cheek, her eyes hidden.

"That's better," Jimmy chuckled. "Let's see you try it on, baby. Show off for me."

He settled back again, and Viyella, marveling at her daughter's womanly guile, caught a look of panic on Jenny Sue's face.

66

"Oh, she best not; might muss it," Viyella said. "Save it for school."

"C'mon Vi, won't harm it none. Always spoiling things." Jimmy shook his head.

"But I *might* hurt it, Daddy," Jenny Sue cried quickly.

"Hold it up to you, sweetheart," Viyella said, and Jenny Sue eagerly obeyed. "That sure is a pretty yellow."

I'm going to have to fix that one too, she thought. Jimmy'll only remember the color. Then, to make it stick in his mind, she added, "Yellow sure does favor you."

Jenny Sue flashed a brilliant smile at them and carefully folded the dress back in its box, out of sight, for her mother to take care of later.

She's nothing but a little girl, after all, thought Viyella.

When school opened, Viyella waved them off down the road, lifting Fella's hand, as she held him in her arms, to wave too. She smiled and called out, "Hold on to H. A., Thomas. Don't spill on your dress, Jenny Sue. Don't forget to eat your lunch, Elizabeth Ann." Then, "Come back, Jee Paw. You can't go with them yet. Right now! Mind!" she scolded, glad to sound a little cross because her stomach had turned to heavy rock inside her, sinking with thoughts of Thomas. "Turn around!" she wanted to shout. "Come home, Thomas." Knowing she couldn't, she panicked a minute and nearly cried, "H. A., you forgot his rope." But, his shoulders squared, Thomas was marching dutifully behind his brother, never looking back. When Jenny Sue skipped out of sight, a flash of yellow at the bend in the road, Viyella longed to run after them before Thomas disappeared too. It's not too late, she thought, one more year and maybe he'll be ready, more like the others.

H. A. stopped for a minute, and Thomas stopped beside him, tipping his head to listen to something no one else could hear. H. A. seemed to be hesitating, thinking about something. Then he waved his hand, dangling way out of his striped shirt, and poked Thomas. In a minute, a wave came from him too. Then they went on. The long pines hid them from view, and they were gone.

Viyella felt as if she had nothing to do. There were beds to make, dishes to wash, the garden to weed, Jee Paw to call to every now and then to check his whereabouts, and Fella to prop against the pine by the window while she hung out the wash. But it seemed like nothing at all with the others away, with Thomas gone.

Jee Paw was always bustling about his own affairs. He'd wave at Viyella casually as he went about his business, the sun bright on his bristly hair, the cowlick a brave feather at the back of his head. Now he'd be hiding behind the chinaberry tree, his face grinning from one side at her where she stood boiling clothes. Then he'd disappear, and in a minute out he'd come on the other side calling "Boo!" and wiggling his fingers in his ears, making Fella gurgle with laughter.

Next he'd streak across the yard, his skinny legs flashing, dust flying out behind him. "Yankees is coming! Charge, boys!"

Fella would stare bewildered, not knowing whether to laugh or howl, and before he could decide, Jee Paw would rush around the corner of the house and skid on the sand in a belly whopper, landing just in the nick of time, with his face turned up and beaming, an inch from the baby's. Fella nearly toppled over with laughter.

Viyella had to laugh too, even while she tried to scold. "Jee Paw, your clean shirt! Now see what you've done."

But it was impossible to be mad. Streaked with dirt, dust powdering his brassy hair, red clay spattering his nose, he would be off again, skinnying up the trunk of a pine, or on all fours, fists pawing the earth, growling up at them. "Grrr! Watch out for the painter. Grrr!"

Or gone altogether, vanished into the field, appearing again, with a piece of dried grass behind his ears and one to chew on in his mouth, only when Viyella called for lunch. He could spend hours in Jimmy's car, just working the wheel. "Rmmmm-rmmmm! Hey there, boys, fill 'er up!" he'd command, his tongue caught firmly between his teeth, his face drawn into a frown of fierce concentration. Then he'd open the door, rush out, inspect the tires, wipe the hood, and with a cheery wave at them, jump in again, slamming the door behind him.

His happiness was contagious. Viyella smiled at his flashing feet, the dirt-splotched shirt flying out behind him, his cowlick like a paintbrush bristling in the sun.

Fella's eyes lighted every time he caught sight of Jee Paw or heard his voice. But that wasn't often enough to keep him happy every minute of the day. Jee Paw wasn't still that long. It was lucky Viyella didn't have much to do.

Because now Fella became a tribulation. The heat hung on, and he was driven crazy with his socks. His face doubled up in anger as he yanked them right off the minute she put them on.

"Mama!" he yelled at her, too furious for tears. "Mama!"

He took to knocking them out of her hand when he saw her approach, and even to knocking *her*. He was big for his age, his shoulders and arms strong as if to compensate for his stumps, and sometimes he caught her a good one where it hurt. Viyella gave up.

But that wasn't the end of it. Fella wanted to walk like everyone else, and he couldn't understand why he wasn't able to. Over and over again, he'd pull himself up on the rocker and start across the room, only to tumble in a heap, the stumps giving out under his weight. Then he *would* cry, beating the floor with his fists, keeping it up, too, until Viyella came to him and held him and soothed him. But the minute she put him down, he'd be at it again.

69

Once he pulled the oilcloth from the table and toppled in a mess of sugar and honey.

"Fella, I can't carry you all day, I can't," Viyella scolded. "You're too heavy and I got work to do."

His lip trembled and he began to tune up; then, smitten with grief and guilt, she picked him up again.

Her back ached now all the time, and at night she was so tired she rushed him to bed, glad he was there, and left without even a song or a tickle. Guilty again, she'd go in to him later and kiss him gently on his fat little cheek. But in the morning it would start all over again.

One Saturday H. A. found some old roller skate wheels on the highway, and he spun them over the kitchen floor to amuse Fella. The baby laughed and laughed and stumbled after them, pulling himself along by his arms.

"Hey, Ma!" H. A. jumped up to find her. She was poking Jenny Sue's pink dress around in the iron bucket, only now getting around to dyeing it. "I got a good idea. How about if I make a cart for Fella? You know, a little thing on wheels to pull himself around by. Then you won't have to be all the time hoisting him and picking him up."

There was a roar from the kitchen, and they rushed in. Fella was banging his head against the stove, trying to stretch his round little arm underneath. Viyella rescued him, and H. A. got the broom handle and swept it under the stove until the little wheels rolled out.

H. A. slapped some boards together that morning, fastened a wheel at each end, and then laid Fella, fighting all the way, down on his stomach and tied him fast with a piece of clothesline. Fella cried and cried, but H. A. placed his little arms over the sides and paddled them along, and soon Fella was rolling. Beside himself with joy, he laughed and made silly noises, calling "Mama! Mama!" for her to see him as he whistled by. If he bumped into anything, the front of the cart took the bang and only added to his joy.

70

Now Viyella was always outdoors chasing Fella, running after the cart to prevent some new disaster—and nothing pleased him more. Exhausted, she'd sink down on the orange crate and let Jee Paw take a turn at running, shouting "Charge, boys!" rushing, then slowing, then rushing again as Fella paddled faster and faster, choked with laughter. At least her back didn't ache so at end of day.

And then H. A. thought of tying rope to the front so she could pull him when she had to. It wasn't half as much fun for Fella, but he accepted it, gazing about happily at everything around him. And when Jee Paw took over, a galloping, runaway horse, or the engine of a big tractor trailer revving up, Fella was beside himself, chuckling and gurgling.

The sun stayed hot and lazy, and the orange crate was warm through Viyella's thin cotton dress. She leaned back against the door and rested and studied on things.

three

IN THE days that followed, when Viyella rested there in the sun, warming her back against the smooth, worn wood of the door, she worried over Thomas. Even though he said nothing about school, when he came home each day he was solemn. Once she caught sight of him around the bend and watched him all the way home. His head was bowed, and not once did he stop and listen for the chirping of birds in the pines or the sounds of the highway carried on the wind across the fields. He just trudged along, stolidly putting one foot in front of the other, until he reached the orange crate. There he sat, chin in hands, most of the rest of the afternoon in H. A.'s taken-up, taken-in old jeans. His eyes were sad beyond his years, and he wore a baffled expression, uncertain, unsure of what might happen.

That was one reason she agreed, against her own feelings, to let him go with Jenny Sue to the highway. It gave him something to do and not so much to think about.

The other reason was Jenny Sue herself. Just this once, Viyella thought, I won't be the one to see that sweet little smile turn down to that hateful pout fixed on me.

But the sense of vague unease and misgiving stuck like a piece of collard green caught in a tooth. You knew it was there, and even going about your business, you waggled it all the time with your tongue to check on it and try to get it out. It didn't hurt, but it pestered.

"*Please* Ma. Let me," begged Jenny Sue. "I'll take Thomas. I'll be careful. I want to help."

She looked as if she really did as she stood there, her arms full of late-blooming ironweed and magnolia leaves. Her lovely blonde hair fell gently over her face, shining against the rich, dark greens. She looked so sweet it took Viyella's breath away; her voice was sweet too.

"I know there ain't much left after all them new clothes and H. A.'s shoes," she said softly. "Let me help; you did before. I helped before."

It was true, she had, Viyella recalled. Years ago, when Jimmy had been off for weeks looking into a job in Winston-Salem, Jenny Sue had picked wild violets, gathered them into the old milk pail, and set herself up by the highway selling to the passersby for whatever she could get. But H. A. had been along with her then to carry the pail and keep track of the nickels and dimes and pennies, and to bring them all, Jenny Sue included, safely home. And it *had* been a help. Few could resist the lovely little blonde girl who sat in the shade, smiling and waving at the cars going by and offering her violets.

There was a big difference between H. A. and Thomas,

poor strange little boy, hardly knowing where he was. Still, Viyella thought, while her eyes searched her daughter's face, I've got to trust her sometime. I can't keep saying no forever.

Jenny Sue became restless under Viyella's look. "Ma," she pleaded again. "Please."

"That's right kind of you," Viyella put in quickly, before she could change her mind and take it back. "Mind the cars. And Thomas. You be careful now, hear?" She smiled and reached to stroke the fair hair. But Jenny Sue was out from under her hand in a second and off calling Thomas.

Viyella bit her lip. Maybe that had always been the trouble, some of it anyway, from the day Jenny Sue was born. Viyella had never had enough time to stand a minute, sit a minute, touch a minute. Always, there was something else to be done quickly, this second. Maybe, she thought, it was because Mama had been there too, to care for, and because the babies had all come so fast. Before she could settle herself to rock Jenny Sue, another one would be calling or crying, or the kettle would boil over on the stove.

And then later, always in the midst of things, always when something had happened, like Jimmy coming home late with the whiskey in him full to overflowing, yelling for his supper; or H. A. falling off the ladder while trying to fix the roof; or Thomas getting loose from his mooring under the chinaberry tree and disappearing—it was always then that Jenny Sue chose to follow Viyella around. She'd twine her arms around her mother and wheedle, "Do you like me, Ma? Please like me."

As Jenny Sue hung on tightly, her fingers clasping her mother's dress, Viyella would snap, "Yes, you know it. But leave me be. Can't you see I'm busy?"

Viyella would disentangle herself from the small hands and rush off to mop the floor, bandage the finger, take Mama her soup.

Later, contrite, she'd search out Jenny Sue, reach for the

little girl to hold and soothe and explain, but Jenny Sue would always push her away, skip off to pester H. A., or start digging her hole to China.

Over and over again, in early evening when supper was either on the stove or just off the stove, Viyella, with a stray minute to spare, would smile at her and try to talk to her and sing to her, but by then Jenny Sue would be nestled in her father's lap or leaning against him as he sat on the orange crate smoking his cigar.

"Go away, Ma," she'd order in her high little voice, "go away."

Viyella's hand would drop to her side, and she'd busy herself over anything that came along.

Jenny Sue hadn't fared much better with H. A. either. She would tag along behind him everywhere, tripping over his feet, tugging on his jeans and whining, interfering with whatever he was trying to do. And having plagued him beyond endurance, she'd run to Jimmy, clasp her arms around his legs, and crying, make up stories. Viyella always had to set things right, just as she straightened the cupboards, putting each pot in its proper place.

"You like H. A. better'n me," Jenny Sue accused her. "You always stick up for him and never me."

"Sugar, no." Viyella had tried to explain patiently. "That ain't so."

"You do, you do!" Jenny Sue cried and ran away again from Viyella's outstretched arms.

It wasn't so, was it? Guiltily Viyella studied on it late at night. Was that what was wrong? But no, she thought, I tried. Oh, Lordy, I did that.

Once, just after Thomas was born, there had been Open House at the school, and for days Jenny Sue had talked of nothing else, planning, extracting promises, and telling them all that was to happen.

74

" 'Course I'm coming, darlin'," Jimmy said. "Wouldn't miss my little girl's party!"

"My Daddy's going to come. Daddy's going to come!" Jenny Sue bragged. "Shall I wear my blue dress with the ribbon on it or the green checkered? Teacher is an old pest. She's got ugly, thick glasses and her nose points at you. But wait till you see my friend Sara Belle! Oh, you'll like her. She wears pretty clothes and she never spills and . . ." she chattered endlessly, as Jimmy laughed and urged her on. Viyella stood apart.

But when the day came, Daddy didn't go. The morning hours dragged by as Viyella waited for him to come get her, but there was no sign of Jimmy. Finally she stopped watching for him. He must have forgotten to pick her up, she decided, so she'd better get going. She washed carefully, combed her sparse hair, and neatly tied it back and twisted it into a tight bun. She clamped an old bonnet on her head to protect it on the way. There had been no planning what *she* was to wear, but the only decent dress she owned, clean and starched, was her old flowered cotton, stretched out of shape at the middle. At least, she thought, the colors were still fast in it.

Viyella lifted the baby onto her shoulder and walked the six miles to school.

Jenny Sue and another little girl were swinging in the school yard when she got there. Thomas was squalling, the bonnet had fallen back around her neck, and loose wisps of hair trailed across her forehead. She could feel the fresh, flowered cotton, stained and sour under her armpits.

"We're here, Jenny Sue! Here we are!" she called, her voice cheerful and proud above the baby's cries. She smiled toward the other little girl as she shifted Thomas on her shoulder. "You must be Sara Belle, Jenny's friend?" Sara Belle glanced at her once, then looked away.

Jenny Sue went on swinging back and forth, her yellow hair flying in the wind, her sweet little face lifted to the sun.

"Hey, Jenny Sue." Viyella's brave smile wavered.

"Sara Belle, go higher!" Jenny Sue swung faster and faster.

"Jenny Sue, I come to the Open House." Viyella had to stand off, away from the flying feet and the soaring swing. Higher and higher they went, the little girls giggling. "Jenny Sue," she began again.

"I hate my ma-aa," Jenny Sue chanted in time with the swing. "I hate my ma-aaa," singsong, back and forth, forth and back, as if she were only counting out one potato, two potato, out goes y o u. "I hate my ma-aaa."

Viyella felt as if she'd been hit by a clod of red clay. If Jenny Sue had flung one at her, it could not have staggered her more.

"Take care," Viyella called after her now. "And thank you, sweetheart, for helping."

But Jenny Sue had gone already and didn't hear.

After a few weeks, Thomas was much happier; there was no doubt of that. Now he came running up the road from the school bus following Jenny Sue as fast as his short legs would go. It seemed sometimes they were in such a hurry they hardly stopped to gather their flowers. Viyella wondered about that but pushed it from her mind and gave Fella extra rides on his cart.

There didn't seem to be very many nickels or dimes coming back home either, but she hesitated to ask. Maybe business was bad. Maybe cars didn't stop so much now that Jenny Sue was bigger. "And this one time I'm going to count on her," Viyella promised herself. "I owe it to her."

Still, there were a lot of queer happenings nagging at her. For one thing, Thomas was making stranger noises than Fella. She could hear him out in the yard, and it made her hold her sides with laughter even as it worried her. She'd sneak to the window and watch, and his gestures would be funnier than his sounds.

He'd frown, chin way down, cheeks blown out, and go "boom-ba, boom-ba, boom," for all the world, Viyella thought, like a big bull fiddle.

He had an old tin can he beat on with stiff pine twigs, drumming away in a steady rhythm, sometimes slow, sometimes quick and intricate, his fingers moving like heat lightning. He'd smile to himself and cock his head sideways, listening to Lord knew what. *What* did he hear? Viyella wondered.

One day her old black comb disappeared, and then she found Thomas, holding it to his mouth, blowing on it for all he was worth. His cheeks looked as if they would burst with his effort, a balloon blown up too full. That must be the fiddles he was imitating, she thought. He could make music out of anything.

Then, too, it bothered Viyella that sometimes Jenny Sue seemed to be munching, but when Viyella stared at her, Jenny Sue's jaws would quickly stop moving. She found a Baby Ruth wrapper stuck up against one of the brick stilts of the house and a broken cola bottle propped against the trunk of the pine. Viyella worried and fussed to herself and one day set out down the road, pulling Fella on his cart.

I'm just taking a walk, is all, she assured herself. I ain't spying, just giving Fella an outing.

But before she reached the highway, she stopped and ducked in the long grass beside the road, hearing already the bull-like noises of Thomas and the rat-a-tat of his tin can. She couldn't believe what her eyes revealed.

A car was drawn up on the soft, sandy shoulder, and the people inside, a fat woman in a print dress and a stringy man in a square straw hat, were clapping their hands and laughing. There was Jenny Sue; smiling and smiling, she bobbed and dipped and pointed her toes, her little feet flying, her pale

77

hair glistening in the sun, her skirt flaring out above her knees. Dancing in the road like the colored children on Muleback.

There was something else, too, that Viyella wished she hadn't noticed, as, quietly and as fast as she could, she hustled Fella home, hoping that this once he wouldn't fuss and that the wheels wouldn't creak. Jenny Sue's little breasts had bounced and jiggled in time with Thomas's music, as high stepping as ever were her feet.

"I can't let on I seen them," Viyella fretted to herself. "I'll have to talk to Jimmy, is all. He'll have to speak to her this time. Can't always be me scolding."

But Jimmy just laughed and slapped his knee.

"Would you believe that?" he chuckled, shaking his head from side to side. "Jenny Sue thought that up? How about that?"

"But Jimmy," she protested. "It ain't right. She shouldn't ought to speak to strangers. Ain't safe, either."

"Aw, Vi, always worrying," he grumbled. "Always fussing. Let her be. She's just a little girl."

She wasn't just a little girl. But how could she explain to Jimmy about the bobbing little breasts, clearly moving through the thin material, when he had his own eyes and still couldn't see?

Then the letter from the sandhills came, from Vinny's store, and Viyella put from her mind the sight of Jenny Sue dancing by the side of the road.

four

VINNY'S HANDWRITING
was big; he'd taken great care, Viyella could tell. He must
have studied over the letter, must have licked the pencil point
many times because the paper was smudged in places. He'd
worked hard, erased, written in again.

"Your Pa is clear in his mind. Was up to see him. If I was
you, I'd come home before it's too late."

Viyella read it aloud, again and again, that night as they
sat by the fire in the first chill of autumn.

"What am I going to do?" she asked every few minutes.
"I crave to see him, Jimmy, but . . ."

"Well, go," he said. "I'll give you the money, Vi." He was
in an expansive, contented mood. The ham bone had been
cooked slowly, with patience; the hoecakes had fallen apart
at a touch. Outside now the stars were sharp, icy cold, the
twigs crackled in new frost, but his fire was lit, his family
was around him. "Trailways won't take much anyways.
Careful to change in Fayetteville, get on the right bus."

As far as he was concerned, it was settled. He hooked his
thumbs in his jeans, leaned back against the wall, and grinned
at them all.

"How can I take Fella's cart on the bus?" Viyella snapped
with exasperation. "Can't put it under the seat, folks would
trip."

"Fella! What you talking about?" Jimmy's chair banged
down hard on the floor. "Fella! What's Fella got to do with
it? You dotty, woman?"

"I can't leave him behind. Who's to look after him?"

"Well, H. A. Let him out of school a bit; won't hurt
none."

"I want to go," H. A. said quietly.

"What?"

79

"I want to go," he repeated.

"What for? You simple-minded too?"

"To see Grampa." H. A. met his father's eyes steadily, his thin face serious and fine-drawn in the firelight, the strong bones highlighted, the chin firmed up now. Viyella, thinking of the little boy trailing after his grandfather to the fields, was suddenly shaken with the realization that he was a man. For a moment he seemed a familiar-looking stranger, someone you thought you'd met before. H. A.'s a *person*, she thought, with feelings of his own. Did he remember after all these years an old man kind to him?

"He should go," she said. "He deserves to. Yes, he ought, Jimmy. Grampa would want to see him too."

"Oh, hell. Woodrow won't recall *him*. Be looking for a little fella if he did."

"Vinny said he was clear in his mind."

"We could take Fella, Ma," H. A. put in eagerly. "I could carry him."

"He's too heavy to carry all that way. He don't want to be toted no ways." With an effort, Jimmy tried to be reasonable, and then the bitterness seeped out like bubbles coming up from the deep muck of the swamp. "Besides, what would folks think looking at him? How they'd hoot at you."

Shem Baker saying, "How about Jimmy Kieffer's last one? No feet. Believe that?"

"His kid's got nothing but stumps. No toes, no bones, just nothing." Jebby Mahon shaking his head and taking another gulp of beer. "Jesus. When I first saw him! Liked to puke."

The laughter, the voices were in Jimmy's head and in the room too. Viyella knew and was silent in pity for his pride.

"Wouldn't want Grampa to see him anyways, now would you?"

Grampa wouldn't pay no mind once he got accustomed to it, she thought, wouldn't care a smidgen after a bit, but she couldn't say it. Poor Jimmy.

80

"It's my Daddy," she said at last gently. "You'd want Jenny Sue to come see you, you know it, and . . ."

"Well, hell, woman, go! I said I'd give you the money. Just be careful."

"H. A. wants to go so bad, Jimmy. Can't fault him for that. It's his Grandaddy, only one he knew."

"Goddam-it-to-hell-sweet-Jesus!" Jimmy got up and strode to the door. "Go, then. The both of you! Hell, I reckon a man can look after one sorry baby and the rest of his family. Go on ahead." And he slammed out the door. The sounds of his footsteps stomping on the hard road on the way to the Bloody Bucket echoed in the still, frosty night.

So it was decided, but Viyella agonized. Maybe H. A. *should* stay home to look after things. Would Fella really be all right without her? And who was going to watch Jee Paw? Make the lunches? She was filled with last-minute instructions.

"Don't forget to sing to Elizabeth Ann at night. Just heat up the pot, Jimmy. Soup's all made to last a while. Keep an eye on Thomas, just the same, even if he's going to school. Mind to see Jenny Sue . . ."

"God sakes, woman, be quiet!" Jimmy roared. "You'll only be gone a day or so."

Feverishly she washed and ironed and cleaned, leaving things nice for them, as if by her very activity she could rid herself of fear. She baked batches of pecan cookies, packing some in the basket under Jimmy's checkered handkerchief for Woodrow, leaving most behind in the old stone crock.

And far into the night, long past his bedtime, Viyella held her baby, crooning; and when Jimmy came to get her, she held Fella more tightly, afraid to let him loose one minute because it might be her last.

She put off going for every reason until at last Jimmy threatened, "You going or ain't you? You best get on your way before your Pa's mind gets fuzzy again." Then, more kindly, "Don't fret, Vi. Jenny Sue will help, won't you, honey? Sure will. Everything will be just fine, you'll see. We'll keep a real pretty house, hey sugar?" He tweaked her hair, and Jenny Sue smiled up at him.

"I can, Ma, I can help."

I've got to trust her sometime, Viyella reminded herself. Got to trust them both.

"Don't worry so, Vi."

But worry she did. She chewed her lips and frowned and fussed at the collar of her best blue cotton dress until it was soiled more by her fingers than by the dust and grime of the bus.

"Oh, H. A., I hope to God I done the right thing," she said over and over.

"It'll be all right, Ma," he soothed. "C'mon, Ma." He pressed the button to adjust the seats and back they slid. "Whoop!" he laughed. "Now forward." He pressed the button again and sharply they jolted upright. But not even his excitement could distract Viyella. Nor the sights to see through the fly-specked window along the way.

"Hey, Ma!" H. A. cried, turning from right to left and back again so as not to miss anything. "Look yonder! Look over there! Hey, Ma!"

But she saw nothing except Jenny Sue dancing in the road, Elizabeth Ann's big, sad eyes, Thomas's mouth squinched up in his noises, Fella whirling on his cart.

"I hope the Lord will forgive me, H. A. I sure hope He will."

"H. A., well I just don't believe it. H. A.," sighed Woodrow. "No, sir, I don't believe it." He whacked his knee protruding from the faded blanket, made a smacking sound by pushing his thin lips together and pulling them apart again, and grinned up at the boy. H. A. grinned back, and Viyella turned away, staring blindly through the thick, barred window at the dull, brown November landscape clipped and organized on the County grounds, lifeless.

Tears, always tears, she thought, disgusted. Useless, no account. Made of tears, I am. She dabbed at her eyes with the sleeve of her best blue cotton and turned back smiling. The pale sun filtered around the bars, striping her still-gold hair and shadowing the high bed where Woodrow lay.

Bars there, too, she thought wearily. And a tough, white harness to tie him in.

"H. A.," Woodrow cackled. "I'll be danged. Hemmy, lookee here! You see my boy?" he called to the toothless old man in the next bed. "H. A., like for you to meet my friend, Mr. Hemmy Tayson. Hemmy, this H. A., Viyella's son I was telling you about."

"How do you do, sir?" H. A. went around the bed and offered his hand.

"Cheep! Cheep, cheep, cheep," went Hemmy.

"Ain't he a fine one like I said? Big tall boy, ain't he?"

"Cheep."

H. A. stood baffled and then slowly lowered his hand. There were two narrow ridges under the white sheet alongside the small hump that was Mr. Hemmy Tayson. They were arms, but they couldn't be moved.

"Glad to meet you, sir," H. A. said gravely, trying to stand and face Woodrow and yet not show his back impolitely.

"Needs filling out, any young'un do, but ain't he a fine specimen?" Grampa bragged. "Vi, I do believe he favors your Mama, yes I do."

"I brought you some pecan cookies, Pa." She rummaged in the basket she'd placed on the foot of the bed. "Wasn't sure they was feeding you good."

"He's a Redfern all right. No doubt about it. Don't see a

smidgen of Kieffer anywhere in him." Woodrow nodded his head proudly. "See that, Hemmy? No shiftless, no-count Kieffer blood."

"Papa!" Hastily Viyella offered her basket. "H. A., maybe Mr. Tayson would like some."

H. A. saw the eager mouth open with anticipation, showing the red, sore-looking gums, and the little eyes darting from the proffered cookie back, hopefully, to his face. He looked to his mother, but she was bending over Grampa, brushing crumbs from his hospital coat, smiling at him as he chomped with pleasure.

"Cheep!"

H. A. broke the cookie, extracted the pecans, and dropped a piece into the open mouth.

"H. A., get me my banjo, son. Let's strum a little like we used to."

There were more pieces to go, held patiently in H. A.'s hand while he waited for the jaws to stop moving, the Adam's apple to stop working.

"Papa, I'll get it. Where do you keep it?" Or is it here at all? Viyella worried as she searched frantically behind the bed and peered under the covers, knowing it was hopeless and not sure whether she wanted to find it or not. It would be as stringless and useless as his withered old voice.

"I need my banjo! 'De time is nebber dreary, if de feller nebber groans. Ring, ring de banjo!' " The words came strong and louder and louder. Woodrow's arms were beginning to flail wildly. "That was Charley's song. Oh, he could tune up, H. A. He could stomp them out! 'I like dat good old song! Ring, ring!' "

"Papa!" she cried.

" 'Rattle of de bones!' " he yelled.

"Hush, Papa, please. Hush." Her voice was breaking.

"Hey, H. A."

"I remember Charley," said H. A. His palm was held out,

84

and Hemmy Tayson's tongue stretched greedily, licking the last bite. "He carried Miss Margaret. Did you tell Mr. Tayson about her, Grampa? Miss Margaret Blueflower."

Woodrow's arms stopped waving in midair and dropped to his sides. H. A. sat on the edge of the bed and leaned forward to listen. Hemmy smacked his lips, and Viyella rested her back against the wall, exhausted.

"Well, now, H. A., Hemmy, was a time this government wasn't so good. You know that?" H. A. nodded his head. "Back before the War, even." Woodrow snorted. "They rounded up them Indians, Cherokees they was, and tried to head them west. Well, now, them Cherokees wouldn't go. No sir. Not the Carolina redskins. Government wasn't going to tell *them* what to do. Went up in the hills, they did, and hid out there. No one chased after them, I can tell you!"

Woodrow grinned, and H. A. grinned back.

"Sneaked right on back down again when the coast was clear. Miss Margaret Blueflower? Folks say she was one. Give us another cookie, Vi, honey. Have one, H. A. You must be hungry after your trip."

Woodrow munched happily. "Good, ain't they, Hemmy?"

Oh, no, thought Viyella. Please no! She glanced apprehensively at the other bed. But Mr. Tayson was lying still, blissfully asleep, his chalk-white eyelids drooped down.

"Pecans. Never did know why you don't make cookies out of peanuts, Vi. Now that would be something."

Before she could answer, he went on, warming to his subject. "I ever tell you what they called peanuts in the War, H. A.?"

"Yes, sir."

"Goober peas, that's what. Lived on them during the War, they did. Would have starved without them. Kept the whole Southern Army alive, know that, H. A.?"

"Yes, sir."

"There was a song about them," Grampa mused. Then suddenly he yelled, "Viyella! Why haven't you fetched my banjo? Let me tune her up to sing H. A. about goober peas. 'I wish this war was over, when free from rags and fleas.' " He sang quietly and mournfully, and she breathed a sigh of relief. " 'We'd kiss our wives and sweethearts,' " he paused and then his voice rose dangerously, " 'And gobble goober peas!' Get me my banjo, girl."

She scurried around to please him, even pulling back the drab gray curtain and fussing in her picnic basket. " 'He says the Yanks are coming!' " he roared, now strumming the invisible air. " 'I hear them rifles now.' Tum tum te tum. 'What do you think he sees?' " He paused.

"Grampa."

" 'The Georgia militia eating goober peas!' " shouted Woodrow. Hemmy Tayson's eyes and mouth flew open at the same time.

"Cheep!" he said.

"Want to hear the Yell, boy? Think I can't give that Yell any more? That what you think?"

"Grampa." H. A. edged up to the bed and put his hand on the old man's shoulder, pushing him gently back. "Tell us about the time Ginril Lee wired all the way to Carolina. What'd he say? I don't recall."

"Don't recall! Why, boy!" thundered Woodrow. " 'God bless those Tar Heel boys!' he says. You know, H. A., those Carolina boys could shoot the puff off a cottontail in full flight at ninety feet!"

"Think of that," murmured H. A.

"And you know we sent more than any other damn, excuse me, ma'am, Viyella, state, in spite of the airs of some?" The calm was short-lived. Woodrow's eyes flashed and he looked about him angrily. " 'Hurrah! Hurrah! for Southern rights, hurrah!' "

86

"Cheep, cheep."

"Vi! Sing! 'Oh yes I am a Southern girl.' C'mon now. Lost your voice? 'Hurrah! Hurrah!' " he bellowed, out of control. Now his knees were churning and his hands waving; the white harness around his middle strained, and neither Viyella nor H. A. could hold him still. The picnic basket upset, the remains of the cookies flying through the air over the room. "Hurrah!"

"Cheep, cheep, cheep!" Mr. Tayson joined in as the nurse came running into the room.

"Vi." Woodrow's old blue eyes were filmed over, and now, as he lay back against the pillow securely tied, his head seemed too large for his body—a newborn baby's head. The skin of his face looked fragile as if it would fall apart at a touch like a cloth worn too long, stretched and washed beyond its strength. Viyella kissed him gently.

"Yes, Papa."

Now the tears flowed down his hollow cheeks, and she was afraid the skin would crumple, dissolve into rags and tatters, wear through to the very bones.

"Wasn't it real nice of these folks to put me by the window, Vi? So I can see out, see my fields." He sighed wearily as the drug began to take effect. "Look how green the cotton's growing." She followed his trembling finger and saw only the dismal browns and grays of late fall. Not even the faint blue lines of the mountains were visible beyond the high stone walls of the County Home.

"Yes, Papa."

"Young fella. Hey, young fella." His quavering voice had lost all authority, and it came out pleading. "We got to go out and get to work. Hear? Time to chop."

"Yes, Grampa."

"So green and ripe. We get at it, hey, son?" He closed his

87

eyes and lay quiet a minute. Then, opening them again, he stared at Viyella and H. A. sitting there, one on each side of him. He smiled. "H. A."

His hand gripped Viyella's. "You come again, Vi, you hear?"

"Yes, Papa," she promised, the tears starting down her cheeks too, knowing she never could.

He smiled again, and his eyes began to close. Then they fluttered open one more time.

"H. A., we got to get those peach trees set in. See how high the cotton is," he said.

"H. A."

five

IT WAS no use to stay any longer, Viyella knew. The next day and the day after that would only be the same: Woodrow lying quiet in his bed by the window, looking with glazed eyes for his fields, or his fire, or his family. And if he saw them, who could tell? H. A. could softly call, "Grampa"; she could whisper, "Papa, I'm right here"; Mr. Tayson could go "Cheep, cheep!"; but Woodrow wouldn't turn his head again. Ever.

Viyella tried to push the bus all the way home. Impatiently she leaned forward, her hands clenched on the armrest, her feet pressed on the floor, as if forcing it to go faster. But it seemed like it took forever anyway, in spite of all she did; starting and stopping at every filling station with a penciled "BUS" sign in the window, at roadhouses just now beginning to turn on their garish lights in early dark, and once, even in the middle of a tobacco field, where an old woman in high black button shoes waved it down with a spikey umbrella. And always people crowding on and crowding off.

The wait in Fayetteville was endless. Viyella scraped up a dime for H. A. to shoot the light machine and hear the ping and click when he scored. He was restless, too, and wandered around kicking the crumpled Dixie Cups and cast-off papers lying on the dirty floor with the toe of his shoe; shoving his hands in his pockets, then taking them out to chew a knuckle; sitting down and getting up again; going to the door to watch for the big headlights and listen for the horn sounding in the night.

But Viyella sat bolt upright, rigid on the hard wooden seat, staring blindly at the torn "Drink Moxie" sign tacked on the wall next to "LADIES" and wondering what was going on at home. What had happened? Was everything all right, the children all put to bed, Fella safely tucked in? Had Jimmy remembered to stick another log on the fire against the autumn cold?

I never should have left, she thought. I'm glad to have seen Papa, glad it pleasured him so to look on H. A. once more; and he liked the pecan cookies, Mr. Tayson too; but it's no count now, he won't even remember. And, oh Lord, is everyone safe at home?

It was black outside now, the red and blue bulbs of the A-1 Cafe, flashing on and off across the street, the only light. No stars. What if there was a storm, Viyella worried, and the roof leaked in on them where they lay? Elizabeth Ann, like the stick dolls she was always nursing, would get feverish, prone as she was to be sickly if she started snuffling first thing in the fall, and winter coming on. What if Jimmy recalled the fire too strong, and it blazed up, catching on to the burlap curtains, and the whole house went up, leaving only the charred chimney for folks to wonder about who lived there? As she had so long ago, on that lonely road back of Vinny's.

Would they all get out in time? Jenny Sue would cry and cling, and Elizabeth Ann would cower back against the wall, in the corner under the iron bed. And would anyone be able to yank Thomas away from his staring, from watching the sight, the beautiful, deadly orange flames? Or pull Fella through the smoke? Fella. The worry of him. The worry of them all.

She sorrowed for Woodrow; she grieved. But there wasn't time or room in her head for recalling days past. Oh, Lord, she prayed, get me home!

It was late, but the Bloody Bucket was still bursting with life and noise, its dim lights gleaming in the black night, when Viyella and H. A. walked wearily up the road. There was a pounding in Viyella's head, and every bone ached with fatigue, every muscle was sore from straining fear, so that the feet she wanted to hurry could only plod in their own time, slowly toward home.

"Go on ahead, H. A.," she urged. "See to things. Don't wait on me."

"Oh, Ma, a few minutes more or less don't matter," he said.

"Might, just might," she answered anxiously.

"It's too dark out here for you to be walking alone." His hard, rough hand grasped her firmly under her elbow, guiding her over the ruts.

"Can't go any faster, H. A.," Viyella moaned. She stumbled and began to cry. They stopped a minute to let her rest before going on.

"Look, Ma!" Around the bend, by the big pine, dimly in the deep night, a flimsy veil of faint smoke rose from their chimney. Light from the kitchen window reached out to them, casting long shadows over the dirt yard.

Viyella ran the rest of the way, tripped on the orange crate, pulled herself up, and shoved open the door.

"I'm home," she sighed, drained by relief, and leaned against the wall to catch her breath a minute before heading to the back room to check her children.

It was warm and snug inside: the fire burning brightly, the hearth swept, the dishes stacked in the sink, the slicing knife hanging out of harm's way on the wall, the kettle on the stove, the table wiped, utensils neatly laid in a row for morning. Viyella took it all in at a glance. There was no time to study it now, but she was pleased.

Jenny Sue did right well, she thought. Aim to praise her good this time.

Then she stopped suddenly and listened. The house was quiet, deathly still. But from her room came, not Jimmy's snoring noises, his grunts and groans and the rustling of the quilts as he fidgeted in his sleep, but funny little tippety-tap sounds, too firm and definite to be mice, too light and irregular for Thomas's drum. She turned and followed them.

"Hey, Ma!" Jenny Sue, wide-eyed awake, danced around the big iron bed, her little feet scarcely touching the warped old floor boards. She wore her mother's nightgown backside to, tied snugly at the waist with Jimmy's polka-dot tie wound tight, the swishing skirts held up by a shiny, glittering pin.

"Jenny Sue!" Viyella cried. "What you doing still up? Where's your Daddy? Where'd you get that pin?"

"Emerald give it to me." Jenny Sue pouted. " 'Cause I'm so pretty, she says."

Emerald! "Jenny Sue," Viyella said sternly. "I've told you and told you not to make up stories."

"Ain't making up stories." Jenny Sue tossed her pale hair. "She did give it to me. I'm pretty."

"Jenny Sue." Then, thinking of the clean, orderly house, Viyella lowered her voice. "You did a good job, Jenny Sue, sugar, leaving things so nice. I appreciate it. Looks real good."

"Oh, I didn't do nothing." Tippety-tap went her little feet, and she twirled away from her mother. "Well, most of it," she bragged. "But Emerald helped."

"Emerald!" Now Viyella cried it out loud. All the fears of all the hours came bursting out in a torrent of frantic, angry words. "Emerald! What was she doing here? Where's your Daddy at? Why ain't he home? Jenny Sue!" Her hand gripping Jenny's shoulder, remorseless, tried to pin the bobbing body, hold it still. "Stop that stepping and look at me. Where's your Daddy?"

The nightgown slid down one arm, the feet tangled in its folds. Jenny Sue stuck her chin up, lowered her eyelids. "Ain't here," she shrugged airily. "Took off down the road. Him and Emerald. La-de-de-de-da." Her feet began to twitch. "Left me in charge. Daddy left me in charge."

"Jenny Sue," Viyella began, but the words died in her throat.

"Ma." H. A. stood in the doorway, a worried frown between his dark eyes. "Ma," he said again. He bit his lip as if uncertain whether to go on, then went to his mother and held her arm to steady her. "Fella ain't here, Ma. Checked all the beds, out on the porch too, for his cart. Ain't nowhere."

"*Fella ain't here?*" Now all the worries came crowding back with a new dread, no, an old one, one she lived with always. "What you mean, H. A.? Ain't here? Fella!" Viyella's voice climbed higher and higher. Wild-eyed, she pushed his hand away and rushed toward the back room where her children slept.

"Ma." H. A. went after her. "Hush, Ma. Go soft."

But she ran about, sliding, stumbling, ranting to herself, and kept calling, "Fella, Fella!"

Elizabeth Ann woke up, clutching herself, and stared, terrified, rocking to and fro. Thomas began to wail; Jee Paw ran to H. A. Even Jenny Sue came in, white-faced, quiet at last, as scared as the rest of them.

Viyella grabbed them all in turn, hugged and kissed them, then was off again, beside herself, peering under quilts and in cupboards, even looking under the stove. She opened the front door. "Fella, Fella." Her voice drifted over the cold fields, weeping.

"Hush, now." In vain H. A. gentled her. "You'll make yourself sick. Fella's all right." He tried being stern. "Ain't under the sink, Ma. Quit, now." But she was frantic, beyond reach.

"Fella's at the Bucket, H. A.," whispered Jenny Sue. "Daddy took him. Left me in charge."

"*What* did you say, Jenny Sue?"

"Left me in charge, H. A.," she repeated, too frightened now to preen. "Fella was hollering and yowling so for Ma, Daddy and Emerald took him along with them."

"*Emerald* took my baby?" Viyella stood stock still, suddenly motionless in the kitchen.

"Daddy's got him, Ma. Fella's all right. Ain't no harm come to him now. Sit down." H. A. pushed her into the rocker, and her head slumped forward on her chest. "I'll go bring him home. You just sit quiet now. Rest, Ma."

But when H. A. headed for the door, she jumped up after him, "I'll get him, H. A., I'll get him." Then she paused a moment as a new thought struck her. "Poor little boy, he'll be tuckered out. And cold. He'll need a coat. Jimmy probably forgot it."

Senselessly she dashed around again and snatched Jimmy's checkered handkerchief, the first thing that came to hand, off the picnic basket, to warm her baby. And then she grabbed the slicing knife off the wall before running out into the cold night.

six

NO ONE
heard her come in. No one heard the creaking door on its
rusty hinges or H. A.'s desperate footsteps racing after her,
nor even her voice, hoarse and plaintive, calling "Fella!
Where are you? Fella!"

And no one saw her standing there either, with perspiration drying, cold now, clammy on her neck in the stifling
heat of the room, her best blue cotton wrinkled and smudged,
her gold hair hanging limp on her thin shoulders, and her
hands clutched around the checkered handkerchief. No
one turned to look at her.

"Jimmy! Where's Fella? Fella, Ma's here," she cried. "I'm
coming."

But her words were lost in the racket at the Bloody Bucket.
The jukebox was blasting to shake the glass out of the
windowpanes.

> *. . . Topeka and the Santa Fe*
> *Here she comes!*
> *Whoo-ooo-ooo*

Over and above the music was the clink of glasses, the scraping of chairs, a high-pitched giggle, the loud voices and
raucous laughter of men with their bellies full of beer, bent
on having a good time.

"Hey, look at him! Hey, lookee there!"

"Send him this way, Jimmy. Gimme a chance!"

"Well, I'll be damned. Look at that little fella go!"

"Heh, heh," came a huge guffaw.

"Count your money, folks, gimme your bets. Two says
he gets to Emerald first."

94

"Hand me a swallow, Shem. Throat's dry, laughing so much."

"Send him this way."

"My turn. How's about my turn."

"You next, Coley. Oooooo-eeeeee!" The voice was gay, brittle, edged with excitement. Viyella knew it.

"Here, darlin'. Sugar, send him here!" The words were slurred together, but she knew that voice too.

Viyella heard other sounds as her ears became accustomed to the roar in the background: the faint little gurgle, the chortle she knew so well, and the squeak of rolling wheels.

The men were sitting around in a circle on the dance floor where on other nights Jimmy and Emerald locked together in step to the beat. Now backs were turned, heads bent, and Viyella couldn't make out what they were watching. Oh, but she knew. She knew.

For a minute she stood stunned, chilled through with fear, her hands cold in the checkered handkerchief, her tired feet turned to ice, immobile. Then she began to run, the sole of one of her shoes flapping loose as she went.

Her eyes were stinging from fatigue and heavy smoke and straining to see, but now she could make them out. Shem Baker tipped back against the wall, a big cigar wobbling between his lips as he laughed. Jebby Mahon hunched forward in his chair, eager, taking quick gulps from his beer can with one hand, the other held out, palm open. Coley Willis slouched on a packing box, balancing his glass on his large belly, his legs lazily swinging as he viewed the proceedings with fat enjoyment. And there was Jimmy, grinning, his hands and knees on the floor, his eyes cutting around at the onlookers. And Emerald, across from him, leaned over, her blouse unbuttoned, falling away, showing a strip of bright pink lace and a dark, deep shadow between her rising breasts. One foot was extended, the sharp toe of the narrow satin shoe pointing.

And rolling toward her, fast, faster, little arms waving, head moving, was Fella, squealing with delight and looking round at each call or laugh with gay brown eyes.

"Mama!" he cried happily, and the laughter and shouts and roars grew.

"Look at him go!"

"You give him a good one that time, Coley!"

"Mama!" called Fella, seeing her and waving a hand. The cart tipped precariously, then righted itself. He chortled.

Shem had sent Fella back, too fast. "Stop! Stop it!" Viyella yelled hysterically, struggling to reach him.

"Mama!" But now Fella's voice was uncertain. Faster, faster went the cart, headed for Emerald's foot. Fella's chest was bumping, one leg was in midair, and his eyes rolled wildly around at them all. They only laughed harder.

Viyella screamed, but Emerald pushed at the same time. With a good hard shove, she sent Fella's cart speeding back across the floor to Jimmy. It was rolling too fast, careening out of control. Now Fella's face crumpled and he began to cry. His body pitched, the cart slanted dangerously, and he yelled in terror.

"Mama! Mama!"

Viyella pushed at Shem Baker, banged into Jebby Mahon's chair, stumbled over Coley Willis' big boot.

"Fella, I'm coming! Mama's here!" she cried.

"Mama!" he called back.

Fella's big brown eyes were blinded by tears. He couldn't see where he was headed, and even so, it was too late; she was too late. His cart smashed into the jukebox, flipped him out like a pancake turning, and crashed over on top of him. The front wheel caught him on his temple and sank in.

The handkerchief dropped; the slicing knife clattered to the floor and lay there glittering. The best blue cotton caught and ripped up the side as, her arms outstretched,

96

Viyella fell forward in front of Fella to shield him. She got there only in time to pull up the old woollen socks to hide his ugly stumps.

In the terrible silence that followed, the jukebox droned on, *Lots of 'em been travelin' for quite a spell*, suddenly loud now in the hush of the room, but Viyella's moaning could be heard above it. Nobody moved but H. A., too late, too, who rushed to his mother and knelt beside her. He lifted the cart off Fella, sent it spinning across the room, and mopped the blood with Jimmy's checkered handkerchief. He sat with one arm around his mother, the other rigid, the palm pressed against the floor for balance, as Viyella rocked and crooned, the baby held tightly against her breast, the battered head pressed close. She smothered Fella's fair hair with kisses, her eyes closed, her face covered with his blood, and sang her mournful, unearthly lament. No one spoke, and the jukebox played on.

seven

STONY-FACED, VIYELLA stood at the small grave just beyond the chinaberry tree. The hole had been dug, the box readied. Beyond the heap of dirt was the marker, only waiting for the earth to settle.

"This one's going to be buried right," Viyella had insisted in her new, strong, unfeeling voice. "Preacher's going to come and ain't going to hurry the words none, either. And Fella's going to have his own place and his own headstone. With his name on it."

"Aw, Vi. He's just a baby," Jimmy protested, but weakly. "Can't put up a memorial to a baby."

"Can," she'd answered grimly.

"If you want." Jimmy sighed. "But what would you mark on it? Fella?" His eyes were filled with tears.

He had apologized, head bowed, voice trembling, explaining over and over. "We was just having fun, Vi. Never meant no harm. Poor little Fella. He was laughing so, Vi."

In some ways it was worse for Jimmy, Viyella thought. Fella ate at him. Now his shoulders shook with sobs, and she, who cried over the twilight settling in, over a blue jay flashing in the sun, over the butterfly wing Thomas had given her, owned no tears at all.

"Would you mark 'Fella Kieffer'?" The tears had begun to trickle down Jimmy's cheek, and hastily he turned his face away.

She was silent.

"Would you?" Jimmy repeated. He was unable to cope with this stern, implacable woman, his wife.

Still Viyella did not answer.

"We could put BABY," said H. A. "BABY Kieffer." His eyes were swollen, his knuckles raw, but where he had gone in the night to weep, she did not know.

She nodded. "Yes," she said. "That'd be fitting."

And so H. A. had carved the words, and in her grief Viyella was as hard as the stone lying waiting.

I am the Resurrection and the Life, saith the Lord . . .

Preacher stood bareheaded. His face was red, wind-whipped in the November cold, but he spoke slowly and gave full measure, even though it was only a child, and a crippled one at that.

Suffer the little children to come unto me . . .

Viyella looked around. Jee Paw clung to H. A.; Thomas was watching the clouds chase across the sky; Elizabeth Ann

98

stood solemn. Nervously, Jenny Sue kept smoothing her bright yellow dress.

He shall feed his flock like a shepherd: He shall gather the lambs with his arms, and carry them in his bosom.

Yes. You do it now, Lord, Viyella prayed. *I* didn't do right. I didn't take care and watch over. Forgive me.

Yea, though I walk through the valley of the shadow of death, I will fear no evil: for thou art with me; thy rod and thy staff comfort me.

And who will comfort me? thought Viyella.

The wind blew a lock of hair across H. A.'s face, and he made no move to push it back, so still he stood, holding to Jee Paw. "Fella couldn't stay on his cart forever, Ma. Not when he got big," he'd said gently. "He's better off now." His voice had broken then. "Anyways, won't have to fret with them socks no more."

" 'Comfort me.' " H. A. was nearly grown now, Viyella saw, as she looked at him standing there so quiet and tall; he'd be going along soon. He was a person, a man, and could never live while carrying too many burdens that weren't his.

We drag him down, she sorrowed, the lot of us. We're going to wear him out, use him up, like that poor old mule Gummy, with too heavy a load to tote. And me the worst. I heap it all on his shoulders, piling it up. Yes, it's coming time for him to go.

Oh, but when he went for good, how would life be tolerable? Viyella mourned. There would still be Jenny Sue, so pretty with her pale, soft hair, like the sun coming out from behind a cloud. But when the sun went under, there were shadows on her face, and would that be all to concern her? Ever? The sun shining on Jenny Sue. What comfort there?

And sweet little Elizabeth Ann, so shy, hiding all hours

in the holly thicket, writing, always writing in her Blue Horse notebook and scampering off if Viyella asked to see it. Scribbling in the dirt when she ran out of paper. Scurrying to bed as fast as she could after supper, pulling the quilt over her head. She could comfort her stick dolls, dressing them in bits of leaves and scraps of old cotton, nurse them, and croon, "Poor baby, I'll make you better." She could line *them* up on the window sill, covering them with her petticoat to keep them warm, or dig them soft beds in the sand and read them her stories from the Blue Horse notebook. Poor babies. But how comfort her Ma?

Little old Jee Paw, cheerfully going about his business, looking from one to the other and then to H. A. for direction. Who would help him? Viyella wondered. And what help would he be with H. A. gone? Later on, maybe, he'd ask himself what H. A. would do if he were here. And then he'd do like H. A. would. But it'd take a while. Years.

And what of Thomas? She could as soon count on him as on the mist over the swamp. And yet. There were the twigs, the bark, the moss laid out for the bird's nest, the bits of string collected, the berries set in the chipped saucer under the window to make it easy for the cardinal to come back.

Viyella's heart ached for Thomas. Too much so? Maybe, she thought. Do I guard him too careful? But who could fault her? Easier to mind Fella and his stumps.

She shivered, stricken by the bitter wind and her own desertion.

Preacher droned on in the cold afternoon. Gone in her own thoughts, she had lost the thread of his words, but the sound of his voice brought solace.

Thomas was smiling at her. She smiled back, heedless of Preacher, Mrs. Parker, or the others who saw. She didn't care who was looking or how her heart was breaking over Fella. It wasn't fitting to smile at funerals, she knew, but Thomas was living. She owed him something too. The Lord would forgive her. And Fella would too. He wouldn't mind; he'd chortle if he was here. If he was here. And how else could she let Thomas know she understood his bird songs, his music, the swishing of pines, his gifts? The songs he played, the songs he heard, once were hers. She moved her lips, "Thank you for the butterfly wing." Only Preacher's voice sounded in the cold, late afternoon. But Thomas knew.

He will not suffer thy foot to be moved . . .

She tensed, glancing at Jimmy, looking round again at them all: H. A.'s new shoes, the dust polished off; Jee Paw's toes wiggling inside the old cast-offs held together with string; Jenny Sue's restless little feet skittering on the hard, bare ground.

Won't have to worry none now about those socks.

It was time for the hymn. They had given up arguing over her choice. It had been Woodrow's favorite, and she was set on it, right and proper or not. It was for Fella and Papa and all who went before and those who were to come.

Now the day is over
Night is drawing nigh . . .

Only Preacher and Viyella knew the words. The others sang embarrassed, hesitant, and their voices were carried off faintly on the wind.

"She put such store on him," Mrs. Parker had said. "Let her do it her way, fitting or not."

Viyella wasn't going to have Preacher speak any false words either, as good intentioned as they might be. What could be said about BABY Kieffer? she had asked. What *would* be said, except "Recall that kid of Jimmy's? No feets. How about that?" And that's how he'd be remembered, she knew, if at all. No one to mourn him in all the world.

Grant to little children
Visions bright of Thee . . .

So that was the hymn sung; and now Preacher was fixing to cast the first earth. His hands shaking, Jimmy lowered the tiny box into its grave, nearly dropping it before it reached its resting place.

We commit the body of this child to the ground . . .

Gently, the dirt fell on the box. "Mama!" Viyella heard Fella call, as surely as she heard the wind lightly stirring the last leaves.

Don't! No! Stop! He's alive! Viyella screamed within; she stood stiffly, silently, her hands clenched at her sides. *H. A., stop them! That's Fella! He's living, can't you see? And his feet will grow!*

"Mama!" she heard and always would.

The Lord bless him and keep him, the Lord make his face to shine upon him and be gracious unto him, and give him peace, both now and evermore.

Amen, Viyella prayed. If that were so. It must be so.

Shall lead them unto living fountains of waters: and God shall wipe away all tears from their eyes.

Jimmy snuffled loudly, Jenny Sue began to whimper, but Viyella was still. *All tears from their eyes and mine as frozen inside as the dirt you lie in.*

Weep all my life for you, Fella. All my life. Now and evermore.

eight

NO ONE saw Emerald at the funeral. Some folks said she wanted to come to express her sympathy for Fella but thought her feelings might not be welcomed. Others said she didn't have any feelings, noways.

Coley allowed as how the sight of the kitchen knife glaring in Viyella's hand had scared Emerald out of her senses and she wasn't about to expose herself to the same sight again.

Jebby didn't think Emerald was afraid of anything: Viyella, the slicing knife, nor the wrath of the Almighty.

"She ain't all bad," Shem said. "She'd want to mourn him, same as any. She was sorry for the little guy, only trying to pleasure him, make him chuckle and be happy while he missed his Mama. And she was sick at how it turned out, real sick."

In any case, Emerald stayed in her cabin beyond the filling station and wouldn't even poke her head out to see if it was raining, morning, noon, or night. She wouldn't answer knocking either. She might even be in bed with the covers over her head, some folks supposed.

Other folks said she just shut herself up, too ashamed to show her face till all talk was said and done and forgetting set in. But Mrs. Parker took care of it. She didn't leave anything to chance and went to call on Preacher and talk it over.

"Can't allow that woman anywheres near, time like this," she announced positively. "Don't let Viyella catch sight of her moaning at his last little rest place. Crocodile tears for sure. What did *she* care? Ha! Not *her* baby! Not her burden to tote. Might think she'd have a regret to carry along with her wherever she goes, but no such luck."

And Preacher nodded his head uncommitted and mumbled about forgive our enemies.

"Huh!" Mrs. Parker slapped her hand down so hard the Bible seemed about to jump off the table. "Forgive! Just don't test Vi's forgiveness right now. Don't let that hussy anywheres near that box or that grave or that house or Jimmy Kieffer neither! Preacher, time you did something about her anyways. Past time. She's been causing trouble round here long enough. Takes two, they say, but not if there wasn't a temptress sashaying about. Ought to suggest a little trip, Preacher. The mountains, maybe, or the city filled with lights, kind of things she'd like to do. Time to move on. Stop hanging around the Bucket and Jimmy Kieffer. He ain't going to notice her now, not for a long whiles. And if he chanced to . . ." Savagely, with pleasure, Mrs. Parker slashed her hand across her throat. "Best Miss Emerald McCullough hightail it out of town. And fast. Ought to call on her, Preacher. You don't, I will," she added grimly.

No one ever knew for certain who did the calling, if any. Some thought Emerald might have been at the funeral just the same, for spite, hiding way down out of sight beyond the bend in the road, a thick black veil covering her face, scarcely able to hear the words or the voices on the wind. Jimmy'd like to think so anyway, they put in slyly.

"Jimmy? You seen him? He ain't studying on nothing these days except to please Viyella."

"Look at him," said Jebby. "Look at Jimmy now. He ain't no great shakes, all humped over, bloat-faced from crying, following Viyella around like he don't know which way to go. Besides, Emerald's wasted enough time on him. Wasn't ever going to get him. Oh, he'd talk with her, dance with her, buy her a beer, and lay her good on her goose-down mattress. But he ain't never going to leave Viyella, for sure, that passel of kids he's tripping over or no. Sure would walk right out and shut the door behind if it was me, but Jimmy always goes home at last, directly."

"Can't fault him," Coley put in. "Ummmm! Viyella cooks up fried chicken, water comes out your mouth just sniffing. Ain't so bad, either, kind of pretty, get a little flesh on her bones."

"Ha! Fat chance of that. Way she works, has babies every time you turn around."

"Ain't got no baby now . . ."

There was silence in the room and Fella was mourned.

So it went, the talk, at the filling station, the Bucket, the Fare Limit on the highway, and throughout the community.

Will Oberton went by to leave Emerald's weekly quart of fresh milk and banged on the door, but she never came to open it and there was no sound within. He went back a week later, and the bottle had frozen in the cold night, burst, and spewed milk and glass all over the porch. Will went off, leaving it as it was. Without his quarter too. She was gone.

No one knew why and no one knew when.

Emerald had headed down the road when the new moon was buried behind a thick cloud, her sharp heels making small marks in the sand which would be mistaken for an animal's, if noticed at all, disappearing by morning. Her suitcase banged against her knee and cut a runner in her stocking. She switched it to her other hand and stood to look her last around the neighborhood. But it was too dark to see; there were no lights anywhere. So she went on.

She planned to hitch a ride to town and catch the bus for Raleigh. Bus wasn't her style, but there'd be trains there, heading through, north or south as the spirit moved. Cotton Belt, Florida East Coast, Canadian Pacific.

Might be back, might not, she mused. But it's no use to wait on Jimmy now.

No use to pleasure herself by smirking at Viyella. Viyella. Her eyes, her terrible voice that night. It had been worse than a dog baying at the moon or an owl hooting in the graveyard. Emerald shivered and turned her thoughts elsewhere.

Oh, but Jimmy, she sighed. You were a man; you sure were. The likes of you don't happen along any old day. I can feel you now, hard, throbbing against me, your sharp teeth hurting so sweet, see the flash of your smile, hear your voice deep in your chest. Jimmy. But there's no use to think on it now, no use at all.

Emerald picked up her suitcase and went on.

A man in a striped tie carried it for her in the station. A man in a lumberman's jacket helped her up the steps of the bus. But her head was turned; she was closed in, far away.

She leaned back in her seat, shut her eyes, and saw the cart, the crazy little wheels, Viyella's face; Emerald shook herself awake. She looked at the blank brick wall framed by the window and saw an old circus poster, grimy at the edges, the clown's grinning face half torn through, and "Alice and Morton" scribbled in chalk, "Nannie Lou Fuller" in brave red paint, the *r* dripping down. And encircled in a lopsided heart: "Jimmy loves . . ."

Now the engine was starting under her chair, rumbling, vibrating beneath the sharp, pointed toes of her shoes. The bus driver came down the aisle collecting tickets.

"How far you going, Ma'am?"

His teeth were stark white under his shoestring moustache.

"Raleigh," Emerald said, and turning her head, smiled full at him.

"Change there?" He leaned against the arm of her chair. "Want a transfer?"

"Reckon not. Aim to take the train on." Lazily she

reached up and flicked her dark hair over her shoulder. "But who knows? Who can tell?"

Route of the Eagles, Nickel Plate Road.

nine

HOW COULD spring be so beautiful? Viyella wondered. Fella was dead. But there it was, so sweet-smelling, the pines so clear-cut against the soft sky, the branches so still in peace—so beautiful it hurt. It promised. And the longing came back, the yearning.

The birds were asleep, their rustlings gone, the wind resigned. Pine needles lay undisturbed; nothing moved; all was quiet. The peace of the gentle night, the still air, the soft smell of spring—so beautiful it hurt.

What is it? Where is it? Viyella wondered. It is the stillness that seeps in, and for a minute you forget.

It was just last year that H. A. brought the baby home. Only a year she had had to know him; only a year she toted, prayed, sorrowed; only a year she mashed gooseberry leaf for poultices, smiled, scolded, cried. And now she had no tears left at all, dried up like Haw Creek in the middle of July.

Yet spring had come around again; the ground had begun to green, the dried-up, brown grass blown away by March winds. Violets poked up in the deep woods, and the sweet smell of pine pollen filled the air. Pussy willows were out, down by the swamp, gentle and furry.

Did I ever laugh? Viyella wondered. A year gone.

And now Jenny Sue was a woman, as suddenly as the redbud bursting into bloom. Spring promised her too.

Often she leaned against the sink, her shoulder higher than her mother's, and as Viyella twirled a dishrag around the chipped cup, her eyes far off, Jenny Sue looked through the window to the last light of day. In the pale sky of early night, the one star enticing, glittering as Emerald's pin, beckoned, sharp and restless.

Jenny Sue shivered, but whether with excitement, hope, or fear, Viyella couldn't tell. The cup was set down in the sink, the dishrag floated in the water, and Viyella wiped her rough hands on her skirt. Hesitantly, prepared for a rebuff, a shake of the head to dislodge the hand, she touched her daughter's bright hair.

But the head came down in the hollow of Viyella's gaunt shoulder, and in silence Viyella's hand stroked the silky hair and clasped Jenny Sue close.

She sighed and Viyella let go, but Jenny Sue made no move.

"Ma," she said. "What's out there? Yonder?"

"Beyond the woods, you mean? Beyond the Bucket and the filling station? The Base?"

"Oh, I don't know." Jenny Sue leaned forward, pressing her forehead against the screen. "Just yonder."

"Well, I ain't been so far, Jenny Sue," Viyella began carefully. "Just to the sandhills and back. Your Daddy's traveled; he could tell you."

"I don't mean purely that." Jenny Sue's body was warm against her mother's, and her soft hair tickled Viyella's chin. Viyella stood perfectly still, looking out the darkening window, unseeing. Elizabeth Ann's lonely train came through the night. "I mean yonder. Where do the tracks go? Where does the highway end?"

"Washington, D.C., likely, one way." She paused a second, then began again tentatively. "I don't truly know, Jenny Sue, what's beyond the highway or the railroad or that star hanging there so bright. Hear the whistle evening time

108

and I ponder it. Always did wonder. You think on it too?" she added, hopeful.

There was silence, and then Jenny Sue fidgeted and moved away. "Going to Washington, D.C., someday," she said firmly, nodding her head. "Yes'm. Sure am."

She was as changeable as spring itself. The moment was over and could never come back. Viyella picked up the dishrag and washed the chipped cup.

Jenny Sue had learned knowing ways to replace the little girl's flirting. Now she swished her long hair back over her shoulder with a practiced and assured turn of her head. Her lips seemed always dewy moist, and her little tongue darted out often to wet them. She crossed her long, slim legs carefully when she sat down, ladylike, so Viyella couldn't fault her; but somehow they were noticed, they called attention to themselves.

Jimmy stared, a patchy red dyeing his cheeks. Then, drumming his fingers nervously on his knee, he looked quickly away at the copper teakettle, the burlap curtains. But his eyes always slid back furtively.

Viyella was certain Jenny Sue knew it, though her manner and her wide blue eyes were all innocence. She flaunted herself with a twitch of her shoulder, a jut of her hip, the second Jimmy came home or Coley Willis stopped by to go coon hunting. And she pestered H. A. the same as ever; always at him but in different ways, more quiet, subdued.

One day she brought home a pink, satiny ribbon, smooth as her fresh-washed hair, glistening as her own little mouth.

"Should I wear it this way, H. A.?" She stood in the middle of the floor, her arms upraised, and held the bow to the back of her head. Jimmy lowered his eyes, and H. A. looked out the window.

"H. A." She didn't whine or command as she used to; she wheedled in a pleading little voice. "H. A. Please. How? Like this?" and as he reluctantly turned his head, she paused;

then with a fluid, graceful motion, she dropped her arms, and quickly, expertly, her hands readjusted the ribbon and tied it, holding back the long, pale hair.

"Dunno," answered H. A., embarrassed.

"Tell me, H. A., please?" Now she cocked her head as she used to, and the shadows from the fire fell softly on her face.

"Dunno." H. A. got up, restless, and headed for the door.

"Jenny Sue, where'd you get that ribbon?" But Viyella's words were useless because Jenny Sue had followed H. A. out. She gave him no peace.

H. A. spent a lot of time leaning against the trunk of the chinaberry tree in the gentle spring air, and Viyella understood his need to be alone. She wondered what his thoughts might be, but then she resolutely put it from her mind, afraid. H. A. tolerated Jee Paw, who often came to stand beside him silently, his hand dropping to brush the stubby cowlick, but when Jenny Sue followed him, he moved off.

Viyella heard their voices late one night when everyone else was settled, when even Jimmy was in bed and asleep under the quilts.

"Don't plague me, Jenny Sue."

"I ain't, H. A. I just want to talk."

"Talk to someone else, then. Sara Belle."

"Oh, Sara Belle!" Jenny Sue snorted. "What does *she* know!"

"What do *I* know?"

"You're a man, H. A." Her voice was as soft and low, cajoling, as one of Thomas's swamp birds.

"Hell I am!" H. A. laughed abruptly, and then there was quiet, the noises of the night the only sounds. Finally he said, gruff but kind, more like H. A., "Go talk to Harvey Willis or Jim Tom Bolar."

"Them! Might's well be Thomas or Jee Paw. H. A., please."

Then the low murmur of their voices blended with the peepers singing in the marsh and the rustle in the pine needles of small, unseen animals. Viyella lay awake beside the hulk of Jimmy, trying to hear above his heavy breathing.

"No, Jenny Sue! No, ma'am, don't you ever!" H. A. shouted loudly. Viyella started, every muscle tense, and sat up at the sound, straining to hear.

"But why not?" Jenny Sue had forgotten her new voice. She was arguing, petulant and shrill. "Ain't no harm in it. He gives me things, pretties."

"No!" H. A.'s voice cracked under the strain and lost authority.

"Reckon you're right. You ain't a man yet." Jenny Sue giggled and Viyella suffered. "Mister Evans J. McNeil is one. Comes by almost every day in his black car to watch me dance. Gonna take me for a ride soon. He says so. Promised."

"Jenny Sue, don't you get in his car."

"Ain't nothing wrong. You're just mad you ain't had a ride in a big new car. The seats are soft and smell so good. Bright red, too."

"Jenny Sue!" Then his voice dropped and hers too, until finally Viyella heard their footsteps on the orange crate.

"Talk to me, H. A., please talk to me," Jenny Sue whispered plaintively.

"I am," he whispered back. "You're being so contrary, is all. I'm trying to talk to you."

It sounded to Viyella as if Jenny Sue had begun to cry, but who could tell for sure?

"If you'd listen to what I say," H. A. began. "Jenny Sue . . ."

Then all was quiet, but Viyella lay awake far into the night. *How to talk to you, Jenny Sue, sweetheart? How?* She closed her eyes. *If you won't hear.*

Neither the warm, caressing air of April nor the sweet, soft songs of night could lull her to sleep.

Though her arms were empty and there was no joy in it, still Viyella rocked in her chair when she had the chance. And Fella was always there, his fat little presence felt just as if she were holding him on her lap; his chuckle, his "Mama!" sounding in her ears when there was no sound but the creak of the rockers on the linoleum floor. She could see him as plainly as she saw H. A.'s shoes, set neatly by the door to spare them, or the first forsythia twig brought by Thomas and blooming in one of Jee Paw's Pepsi Cola bottles. Memories of him were always with her, even when her thoughts went constantly back and forth, forward and back, like the rockers going nowhere as she pondered Jenny Sue.

Once, twice, three times, so often had she tried to speak to her, ending helplessly and futilely when Jenny Sue had interrupted and, smiling prettily, had begun to chatter.

"Know what Sara Belle says, Ma? Says at the end of school she's going to have a real party. Ice cream and everything. With boys, too. Going to ask H. A. And we all put on something pretty, not a school dress. What'll I wear? Can I get something new, Ma?"

Or: "Oh, Ma, I can't talk serious now. Did you know if you rolled pieces of your hair tight around old rags and let them sit awhile, they'd curl? Got some rags you ain't needing for quilts, Ma? Can I try it please?"

Then the door would bang carelessly behind her as she sought out H. A. by the chinaberry tree.

Well, maybe H. A. could save her. From what, Viyella didn't know, wasn't sure, but she was deadly sure there was something all the same. He'd have to. There was no one else.

A snake slithered out one day from under the house and lay still as air on the needles beneath the pine. It looked like a long thin stick, and after a while Viyella began to think she was wrong, that it *was* a long thin stick. But she knew. And worse, the chickadee perched on the branch, the winter bird, lost a long way from his home, knew too, but he stared just like Viyella. His eyes bright and curious, he hopped down to the next branch, and then the next and the next, lower and lower. The snake never moved any more than Viyella, who watched in horror and fascination. But she knew he was looking the little bird down, with an eye like a bit of dark glass. The chickadee jumped on the ground and cocked his head, questioning. Nearer and nearer he came, and the snake never moved. When he drew close, at last Viyella shook herself awake.

"Watch out!" she screamed, flapping her apron. "He'll get you!"

The snake's head stretched out quicker than Jee Paw could snap a rubber band. The chickadee hopped, hysterical, his wings beating crazily. Then he was off, out of reach.

Viyella leaned on the window sill and covered her eyes. "I saw him. I knew he was there waiting, enticing, and even so I was just about too late."

She wouldn't rest until H. A. drove the snake from his hiding place and stomped him.

Lingering at the sink asking for help with the dishes, Viyella waited patiently for Jenny Sue to come close again. But though Jenny Sue stood beside her drying willingly enough, the hollow of Viyella's gaunt shoulder was never filled again with the bright head, her hand was never allowed to touch and hold.

Once Jenny Sue came near while she was stewing some old chicken bones.

"Ma," she said, "I watched you do that so many times and still don't know how."

"Boil the water is all." Viyella kept her head bent and her hands busy poking the carcass. "Seasoning's what makes it good."

"How do you know what to put in? Or how much?"

"Little of this, little of that. Savory. You learn. Taste a

smidgen from time to time while it's cooking. Put in a bit more. Got to be careful—not too much right off. Soup would spoil."

"Oh," said Jenny Sue. "Got to stand there all that time sampling? When do you know it's done?"

"Got to keep an eye on it, go slow. Soups can stew along. Ain't never purely done, always could be better, stand more of this or that. Can't let them boil away entirely, leaving only bones. So you watch and dip in the finger, and if it tastes right, then it's done, good as you can do."

"Oh."

" 'Course some soups are better than others." Steam rose from the pot, curling the loose ends of Viyella's hair round her face. "What you got to start with counts, and then how much care, watchfulness. You take my meaning, Jenny Sue?"

But how could she when Viyella wasn't sure herself? Anyway, Jenny Sue had gone, there was the slam of the door, and Viyella finished by herself, running for a cloth as she heard the hiss of the water boiling over.

Along about then Jenny Sue came home wearing a tight, black, short-sleeved sweater.

"Say, that's real pretty, sugar." Jimmy whistled in admiration.

"Ain't it hot?" asked Jee Paw.

"Could I have it someday, Jenny Sue? Later on, I mean," Elizabeth Ann begged, "when you get bigger."

Lord save us from that! thought Viyella, but before she could say anything, Jenny Sue whirled, her tiny feet doing her little dance steps. "Don't you like it, H. A.?"

"Maybe Elizabeth Ann should have it right now," he mumbled, his face guarded.

"Oh, H. A.," she pouted, but the corners of her mouth twitched in her secret little smile. "You like it, Thomas, don't you?"

Thomas looked around, beaming at them all, then turned back to Jenny Sue. Viyella opened her mouth to speak, but Jenny Sue's light, dancing feet stopped in front of her mother as she pulled down the ribbing where it had arched up over her petticoat.

"Someone give it to me, Ma."

"Who?"

"Oh, someone," Jenny Sue answered airily, smiling off into the distance.

"Who?"

"Who cares?" said Jimmy. "Goes with her light hair."

"Was too small for them, see, Ma?" Now Jenny Sue frowned, earnestly explaining. "Didn't fit no more, couldn't even get it on. So I got it." She fingered the thin wool. "Pretty, ain't it? It was too tight for them, Ma, you know."

"And it's too tight for you too, ma'am!"

"Oh, Ma." Jenny Sue began to sniffle.

"Viyella, c'mon."

The black wool clung. Jenny Sue's shoulders were narrow and her waist so slender H. A.'s shoelace could go around it and tie. But between them, Jenny Sue's breasts rose, full and womanly and firm, like the rounded ends of summer squash, ripe for picking.

Outlined in black, calling attention to herself, she wore the sweater every day, even when the afternoons turned hot and the sun began to burn.

Viyella spoke out about selling the flowers.

"Seems to me you'd be tired of it."

"Oh, no, no!" protested Jenny Sue. "It's fun! And there's so many now, violets and dogwood . . ."

"Ain't right to pick dogwood," scolded Viyella. Oh Lordy, what did that have to do with it?

"Just a little, Ma, not enough to hurt any. Folks like it. And Thomas knows how to snap it so it don't hurt the tree none. Don't you, Thomas?"

Thomas grinned and puffed out his cheeks in preparation for his tuba thumping noises.

"We're getting by now, Jenny Sue; we don't need extra. Don't you want to go to Sara Belle's after school? Maybe Daddy could come to carry you home?"

"Oh, Sara Belle." Jenny Sue sniffed. "And Thomas likes to so much. He ain't got nothing else to do. Poor little Thomas."

She knelt down, putting her face close to his. His cheeks caved in, and he looked up at his mother, beseeching.

"Ma?"

"Oh, Thomas," Viyella sighed. What else for him to do? Poor, queer little morsel. Life would be hard enough. Still . . . "Jenny Sue," she said firmly, "you don't have to care for Thomas. I thank you kindly, but . . ."

"Please, Ma. I like to."

Thomas looked from one to the other, afraid. His lip trembled.

She'll tire of it for sure, sooner or later, Viyella assured herself. Sun gets hot and lays that sweater flat against her back and her legs start to drip, she'll weary. Can't tell her I know she's dancing. Ain't *supposed* to know. Can't forbid. Jimmy'd only laugh and say, "Where's the harm?" Can't do nothing but trust. Have faith in the Lord. H. A. Ain't nothing else to do.

And then one day Thomas came back alone, his eyes wide with fright, his mouth working, his fingers clasped desperately around some wilted daffodils as he tried to hold their tired, droopy heads still in his shaking hand. It was late, supper was drying on the stove, and only a scarlet rim of sun hung briefly over the dark line of woods.

"Jenny Sue went!" he cried. "I waited and waited, and she didn't come back." His words, intermixed with sobs, tumbled over themselves so Viyella could hardly understand. But she knew.

"She said she'd come back. She promised." The effort to tell his story was too much. His face broke up in pieces, his shoulders heaved violently, and Viyella bent down and held him to her, offering such comfort as her lean body could.

"Shhh, Thomas, don't cry."

"She left me there!" His voice was muffled now by her worn cotton. "All alone. And I waited and waited and cars came whizzing by and all the flowers are dead."

"Where'd she go?" asked Jee Paw. One by one the children had gathered around, watching solemnly.

"Big black car . . . man give me a Milky Way, but while I was watching and waiting it spilt in the sun," Thomas wailed. "Spilt on my pants. I'm sorry, Ma, I got it on . . ."

"Shh," soothed Viyella and kissed his cheek. The sticky chocolate was bitter in her mouth. "It's all right, Thomas, all right."

"We should go look for her, Ma," said Elizabeth Ann. "She can't see in the dark. But I can. Lots of times I write after the fire's down, and I can make the words out real good. I can find her, I bet. We should look for her right now. Maybe she's lost."

"If she's lost, she'll find her way home." Viyella held Thomas tighter. "She's grown up now, Elizabeth Ann. She'll come home, sweetheart."

"We better go look for her, Ma," urged Jee Paw. "I can see in the dark too. Once I thought I saw a painter in the road, but I could make out it wasn't, just a possum. No moon out either. We better go look for her, Ma. Shouldn't we, H. A.?"

Viyella looked up, and her eyes met H. A.'s and held. It wasn't any use to look for her. None at all.

"She'll come back," she said to the children over and over again later in the week. "Any day now, she'll come back."

But God-a-mighty, how to tell Jimmy! "Be home soon, I reckon," she promised him. "I look for her any day now, rounding the bend in that pretty, black sweater. Sun shining on her hair."

But the days went by, and soon the children stopped asking. Jimmy's fork fiddled with his food, his face went slack, and heavy lines drew down his mouth. At night H. A. leaned against the chinaberry tree, looking down the road. Once Viyella heard him cough, a terrible, tortured noise. But that was all.

A card came from Raleigh: "Ma, I done wrong. I know it. I'm sorry." The ink had blurred, but Viyella could make it out.

And then another one from Winston-Salem: "I'll come back home. Your daughter Jenny Sue Kieffer."

In June there was a picture of Robert E. Lee, from Richmond: "Thought maybe H. A. would like to see the Ginril. Ma, don't worry none. I'll try to get home."

A long time passed, and it was August, with the sounds of the cicadas stinging the air, when the next card came. From Washington, D.C.: "Ma, you should see it here. It's so pretty. Tell H. A. hello from Jenny Sue."

And then there was nothing.

ten

NOW LIFE became unendurable for H. A. and Viyella. There was no consoling Jimmy. He could no more get rid of his grief and loss than the skies could clear themselves of the heavy clouds before hurricane season was done or the September rains stop dripping from the porch roof.

There was nothing Viyella could do to please him but hustle around at his bidding, cringe at his oaths and sudden, angry hand, shoo the children out of his way, and shush their least sound. He still had the good sense not to mention Emerald, and he couldn't speak of Fella, but he moaned over Jenny Sue, mumbling to himself. If Viyella tried to sympathize and soothe with her touch, he'd flash her a look of angry hatred and push her arms away. So she went about, tight-lipped and tense, cooking, cleaning, always with a wary eye out for his presence.

The nights were bad when he came stumbling home, crashing into the orange crate, banging his head on the door. It came up and hit him, he complained, and she was to blame; she was to blame for the endless, ceaseless drizzle, the sea of mud that was the yard, the whole gray world around them. Her fault, all of it. And all the rest, too.

The days he didn't go to work were the worst. He sat hunched up by the fire, a bottle of redeye between his knees, but it brought him no solace. His head would jerk up, his jaw jut out, and he'd glare at her through mean-looking slits of eyes. Viyella became afraid. There was no telling what he might do next, what ugliness might stream out of his mouth, what violence might spring from his body.

Viciously, he kicked her rocker where she sat. Once it splintered and only barely did she catch herself in time to keep from falling onto the rough, spiked edge. He roared with laughter, pointing at her as she picked herself up.

"Heh, heh, heh! Didja see that?" Driblets of liquor trickled from the corner of his mouth down his unshaven chin and onto the dirty shirt collar he hadn't changed since two washings ago. No one else was in the room, but she couldn't say, "Who are you talking to, Jimmy?" He'd take it as a challenge and rise up to hover over her, menacing, shouldering her against the wall, demanding, accusing, bullying, until she took it back, whatever it was she'd said.

So he sat there, addressing the empty room. "See that? Heh, heh!" And laughed fit to kill.

Now Jimmy's car lay in the patch of field beside the house, its wheels sunk in mud. Each rain beat on it, rusting it, and the hurricane winds sweeping in from the east, blowing salt from the sea before them, corroded it. Hail attacked, pelting the dented tin. A flying limb struck and the windshield cracked, bits of shattered glass scattering over the worn upholstery. And inside the house, Jimmy sat, desolate.

He did the best he could, Viyella reminded herself, when his foot was always itching him to wander and his eye looking around. And who could fault him? Look at me, withered old thing, dead stalk of corn in the heat of summer. Emerald had satisfied something he craved, something he lacked. Emerald was his mirror, and he didn't know who he was, now that she was gone. He couldn't see himself as the gay, swaggering Jimmy Kieffer.

The money disappeared out of his pockets as fast as it came in. Clattering and squalling greeted him when he came home at night, weary, to rest in his house. The curtains flapped at the window in storms, flies tickled, pestering in summer, snow hissed down the chimney on his fire in January, smoking up the room. And always the noises, the hollering, the piping voices. And mine not so soft as might be, Viyella thought sadly.

He doesn't understand us, she mourned, none of us. Fella and his stumps, poor, queer little Thomas, Elizabeth Ann always keeping her distance, Jee Paw hanging on to H. A. And H. A. was purely a mystery to Jimmy. Jenny Sue was the only one close, the only comfort he had; Jenny Sue was his heart, and now she was gone. Poor Jimmy. And his car

120

lay rusting in the hurricane winds and dreary rains of September.

Taut, held in, her own grief repressed, Viyella went through the days with the fear dancing along her nerves like so many mice skittering up and down wires, biting and gnawing with their little teeth.

Not so H. A. He began to answer his father back, his voice quiet, but angry too. He was big now, filling out in the shoulders, and Jimmy's hand didn't dare strike out at him. That made it all the worse. Bottled up like a too-tight lid on a teakettle, the steam would blow off in a rush of words. He would lash at the boy with his tongue.

"What the hell you think you're doing, eh, H. A.? How come you think you know so much? You're just a snot-nosed kid."

When H. A. fixed the rocker, Jimmy knocked it to smithereens all over again, complaining, ranting, making fun of the work. When H. A. built the fire, Jimmy kicked the logs so ashes smothered the flames, and railed at him.

"H. A., you look like a skinny-legged jack rabbit."

"Hey, H. A., that a haircut? Seems like someone took the shears to a frisky lamb."

"Your skin's as pebbly and bumpy as Muleback Road in a dry spell. Ha! Swear if it ain't so!"

Nothing H. A. did was right; nothing was right about the stupid son of a bitch anyways, Jimmy proclaimed.

The day came when H. A. had had enough.

"Ain't going to talk that ways to me," he said.

"Who says I ain't, hey? *You?*" Jimmy sneered. "You? You skulking, overgrown, mule-eared . . ."

"Ain't right to slander Ma, neither." H. A. stood firmly, his only movement a twitch in his thin cheek.

"Ma! Your Ma! Heh!" Jimmy made a rude noise.

121

Now it seemed H. A. would shout or cry in anger and raise a hand, but he stood unbending. "You belong in the back house," he said to Jimmy, the biting scorn in his voice held back by gritted teeth.

The bottle was flung across the room, whistling by H. A.'s head, missing by inches; still H. A. stood, his eyes never leaving his father's. The bottle smashed against the window; the glass, breaking along with it, fell in a shower, and the rain poured in to mix with the whiskey, staining the wall.

Enraged, Jimmy flung himself toward H. A., and then as suddenly, he sank down again. He buried his head in his arms, and his shoulders heaved in sobs. This was more terrible to Viyella than any ranting and raving. This was Jimmy, once arrogant, dashing, masculine. This was Jimmy, this sodden mess.

Strung tight, near to breaking with terror and pity, she whispered, "He ain't right, H. A. Go soft."

"What's that you say, eh?" Jimmy looked up, his eyes puffy and swollen, his tear-stained face streaked where the drops had washed away the grime. "Always whispering, you two. Always conniving against me, talking behind my back. Think I don't see? Think I don't know? Always holding yourself above me, better'n me. Just like all them Redferns, stuck on theirselves, snooty, too good for the likes of me."

For a minute he became belligerent, scowling. Then his head dropped forward again, and dreadful strangling sounds emerged from his throat. "Never did take to me, any one of you. Never did. I want my little girl back," he sobbed. "Oh, Jesus, give me my little girl back. Send her home. I want my little girl to come home."

H. A. stood without expression, looking at his father.

"He ain't right since Fella died and she went away, H. A.," pleaded Viyella. "You know that. Ain't right at all."

"My little girl liked me," Jimmy blubbered. "She liked me. Why did you drive her away. Why?"

"I didn't drive her away," H. A. answered steadily.

"Beating on her, picking on her." Now Jimmy began to holler, the shrill noise scraping along Viyella's nerves, the mice scampering frantically, jabbing everywhere. The wires snapped.

"H. A.!" Viyella cried.

"You didn't favor her, you and your Ma. She knew it, oh yeh, she knew it, she knew you didn't like her."

"I did too like her." Now H. A.'s voice was beginning to crack. He'd stood stiff for too long. Furtively he dabbed at his own eyes with his shirt sleeve. "I did too," he repeated hoarsely, defensively. "Better'n you. You just treated her like one of Elizabeth Ann's stick dolls to play with, only you didn't take such good care. You just didn't know."

"Ha!" Jimmy forced a laugh and pointed a shaking finger in his son's face. "Look at him! Look at the big man now!"

"You didn't know," H. A. repeated doggedly. "You don't know anything. You're just a drunken bum anyways!"

"H. A., don't!" The fear grew to bursting, exploded into hysteria. "Don't!" Viyella cried again, no longer sure of what she meant, but terrified and having nowhere to turn. "Don't plague your father so!"

Stricken, H. A. turned to look at her, his face more torn with pain at this betrayal than at his father's sudden jeering laugh. As if she had hit him, his own dark eyes filled; and shattered, he ran from the room to lick his wounds and to heal, away from them all.

Where he went, she never knew. Likely down to the swamp to lean against the thick, strong trunk of the old oak and throw small stones as hard as he could into the murky pool at its roots, watching the splash they made, the circles widening until they disappeared in dark shadows. Or maybe way back in the woods to the old turpentine camp, collecting dried twigs along the way to make a fire to warm himself. His clothes would be wet through, she worried, and he'd be cold. Or maybe he just went down to the filling station and scrounged up nickels to play the pinball machine, laughing loudly, looking and whistling at the girls going by in cars, building himself up again.

Viyella didn't question. It was right; it was coming time for him to go.

Jimmy slept for hours and hours, stretched out so wide on the iron bed there was no room for her. One arm was flung back and the other covered his eyes, though Viyella hastened to nail up a flour sack at the window to darken the daylight. Tremendous snores came from his nose, wheezes, like Shem Baker's pump on the blink. His mouth hung open, and dirty juice trickled from the corner onto Viyella's quilt. Sometimes his legs thrashed about restlessly, but mostly he was still, dead still, the rise and fall of his belly in time with his heavy breathing the only sign of life.

He was asleep when his son came home. H. A. went to the door and stood a minute, looking at his father with disgust. He didn't go again.

When Jimmy woke, he sat morosely at the kitchen table, doodling with some sugar spilled on the oilcloth, now making little hills, now flattening and tracking his fingers through in tiny roads or swirling, meaningless letters. He didn't speak, and that was a relief, and he barely glanced up when Viyella brushed by doing her chores.

But H. A. didn't look at her either. Not directly. He went quietly, fetching and carrying and helping, but his eyes didn't see her. It crushed her, stabbed her as surely as she dreamed she had knifed Emerald. I'd rather *be* Emerald, lying on the floor with blood staining my satin dress, Viyella thought. That was a wound you could see, an outside wound. It was inside bleeding that was dangerous. Inside bleeding was what killed. Your love mowing you down.

But H. A. didn't see her. Please look at me H. A., she

begged silently. *What was it I done to you?* Over and over she worried it in her mind: Jimmy's nasty laugh, his head sunk into his shoulders. H. A. standing there so tall, and then crumbling, his control gone, not nearly so manly as he thought or tried to be, a little boy defeated and ashamed to have her see him so, running from the room.

But what did I do that was wrong, H. A.? she wanted to ask in her anguish. *There I stood, wiping my hands on my apron, not knowing what, but knowing it was something, knowing I was to blame. Your brown eyes were so fierce and desperate and angry, your jaw set, the veins in your neck standing out with hate, and all I ever did was love and pray and hope, like now. Hope for the sun to come up again in the morning and my cardinal to come back and you to understand. Can you, H. A.? Or is your love wrecked too? Get out before your hope is.*

No, don't! she nearly cried aloud, as if H. A. had already rolled up his things in his old striped shirt and was hiking down the road in the September mist. *Stay. Let hope be killed.* Be glad it's a streak of lightning striking the chimney top and not the tumbling of bricks one by one in each rain that falls.

It was too much, she knew. He'd be fettered, bowed down with all their troubles, crippled worse than poor little Fella. Her eyes followed him, worried and afraid. He'd be going along directly. *But not yet, H. A., please,* she pleaded silently, *not yet.*

"Ma." He stood before her and now he *did* see her; his dark eyes looked directly into hers. "Like to say I'm sorry Ma. Like to . . ." He stopped, and his large, clumsy hand reached out and closed quietly on her thin shoulder.

Viyella, struck dumb with fear and dread, knowing, couldn't move. Her own eyes held his.

125

"I'm going on, Ma," he said.

She nodded.

"Send you what I can."

There he stood, half boy, half man. "Save yourself," she whispered. "No use here. Save yourself."

He didn't seem to hear. He looked all around the room, memorizing the copper pot, the burlap curtains, faded now, the fireplace, where he had laid logs and pine cones for her to light tonight. Then his eyes came back to her face.

"Aim to watch out for Jenny Sue," he said. "Send her on back."

"Lord willing," she sighed. "I hope so. Thank you."

"Say goodbye for me, Ma. Elizabeth, Thomas, Jee Paw." He stumbled over the names, and now he couldn't go on. He lowered his head.

"Hold yourself proud, H. A." Her voice was as steady as her eyes on his thick, bright hair. She lifted her chin. "Hold yourself proud."

"You be all right? You get along all right?"

"I'll get along."

Swiftly he bent and kissed her cheek, and then he was gone.

She stood motionless a minute, then ran to the door, calling after him. "H. A., wait! Wait, H. A.!"

He stopped and turned back, and Viyella darted to the sink. From underneath, tucked behind the box of Twenty Mule Team, she drew out a coffee can, and quickly, surely, her fingers found the nickels and dimes, hoarded, saved against this day. Under a dampened shred of Jenny Sue's old red dress lay waiting the biscuit and slab of ham she had already wrapped for him. She gathered it all in her apron and met him under the chinaberry tree.

"No back talk now," she said, thrusting it at him. "Take it, H. A. You mind."

And before he could protest, she had run from him up the path.

She watched him out of sight down the road as she had so many times before on his way to school. But she'd always known then he'd be back that afternoon, Jee Paw rushing out to meet him, running, jumping at his heels like Shem Baker's new puppy. Fall and winter and spring. And summer too, when he'd sauntered down to the highway sometimes and hitched a ride to town to run an errand for Jebby. But then he'd be back directly, before the sun lowered down behind the pines. When would he be home again now?

Viyella hung back behind the curtain in case he turned around, looked homewards.

He stopped once, hesitating, as he had so long ago while leading Thomas out into the world, and she drew the burlap over her face, hiding.

When she looked again, H. A. was heading around the bend by the big pine, and he held himself proud.

part three

Thou hast put gladness in my heart.

PSALMS: 4:7

one

AS SURELY
as the moon rose, its cold, sterile light gleaming on the barren
pine flats, Viyella knew she would have no more babies. The
dress snug at the waist, even early on, the quick jumping
from the table to the back door just in time, the involuntary
secret smile when pondering on who was to come, what kind
of person, the heavy, lazy lumpishness at the end, and the
wonderful fatigue when it was over, bathed in satisfaction
and the feeling of accomplishment (short-lived as it might
be), were not to be hers again. She hadn't stopped to think
yet whether she was glad or sorry. The fact was there, waiting for her time and consideration. Like an aching tooth, if
she put her finger on it, the pain might stab her, or it might
give relief. Later, someday, she would probe.

But she was much too young for this crazy time of life.
Much. When women were silly for no reason at all.

Mrs. Betts had taken to dancing in the church vestibule
to the sonorous strains of the old off-key organ, her tiny
feet spinning in their square stubby shoes, the round red
cherries nodding on her straw hat.

And Mrs. Peddy, bitter and ugly, her mouth turned down
in revenge against the world and all it had given her, fighting
too, hollering and screaming at Frankie for wiping his mud-
dy boots on the carpet, when what she really meant was his
wandering brown eyes jumping out of their corners at the
little girls all in pink. She, who never raised her voice before
except in Hallelujah in the Christmas Choir at Centertown
Church.

Or Mrs. Podents, sitting there with not a light on even in
the dark, crying and moaning far into the night, her hand
on what was left of her breast, where no man's hand, not

131

even Col. Podents', had ever been, and now it was too late.

Viyella tried to recall Mama at this age; she remembered her out in the fields, whistling.

Maybe age has nothing to do with it, Viyella thought. I'm much too young, as years go. But who could tell how old the womb, how tired and worn out? Who could tell how aged the body? Of course there were wrinkles and such. Thinness or fatness as the case might be. But who could tell how old inside?

Maybe the old women whispering at gatherings, shushing when anyone came near, were right. Maybe they knew, more than anyone, what a body'd been through. And how old you were didn't matter no more than the wind flicking round a stone. If it's coming, it's there; that's all there is to it, Viyella decided. Don't matter what age it's supposed to come; it comes when it's ready, like a baby. Women. Crazy is all. Commence to talk to the broom. Cry at the wisteria vine. No particular age. Who knew?

There the ladies sat, she'd seen them, with hats on and not talking proper. Where had they learned those words? Viyella wondered. They slapped their knees and laughed, cutting their eyes. "Uh-huh," they agreed, heads nodding in sympathy, "that one's done. Don't know what's ahead of her, poor soul."

"Used up."

"All the signs."

"So young, too."

"Ain't no telling what wears out first. I mind me of our old mule Gummy. Always putting his right front foot down when he didn't know the way in danger. That foot bent double, gave out, so much use. Had to shoot him."

"They should shoot *us!*"

Hee, they laughed. Hee, hee, and they all began to talk at once.

132

"Did you ever think . . . ?" and "Did you ever get the idea . . . ?"

"Did you ever cry for no reason but the sink was full of dishes and it was after dark?"

"My Mama, she put the teakettle on at two o'clock, and every day it spitted and sputtered and burnt itself out. And in she'd come, asking 'Who left that kettle on? Do, Jessie! Who put that kettle on, spatting so?' "

"I mind the time Emma was sitting with me in the parlor, cold, gusty day out it was too, and she got so hot she like to roast in an oven. So finally she says, 'Lulie, you mind if I take off my dress? I'm burning up.' So off it comes, and she's sitting there sipping tea with her little finger curled just so, way she does, and in comes Preacher! In her petticoat, she was. Needed darning, too."

Hee hee, they giggled.

"Ever get scared you'll throw the poker at your old man? If McLellan Brown comes into my kitchen one more time burping and scratching his stomach, Lordy, I'll do it!"

They cackled, and the logs popping in the corner fireplace accompanied them. But they knew. Age had nothing to do with it, when a body was used up, done in.

If Mama were alive she could tell me about it, Viyella thought. I'm just plain crazy. I think this, I think that, and it ain't none of it so. But I'm too young anyways, and I haven't time to study it, she decided.

When she had too much time, that was all she had.

Now even Jee Paw had set out for school, his cowlick slicked down with water but staying put only till he reached the bend; then she could see, even at that distance, how, sundried, it bounced up again. He marched on, never looking back, his shoulders held so straight, his shiny new shoes set firmly down on the sandy road, and twice he poked Thomas, urging him on, no dawdling.

So there he went with the others, the last of the line, and the house was empty, still, with the unnatural quiet of nobody living there. And here she was, Viyella, with no time to ponder on it, no time at all. She was much too busy.

Not even a knee baby to chase, she thought.

And where was Jenny Sue? Pray to goodness whoever she's with listens to her wheedling, treats her kind, strokes her pretty hair, and calls her "sugar." Hope she has her new dresses and pins and whatever else it was she was looking for when she set out.

Where did I go wrong, darlin', where did I fail? Viyella punished herself.

But she was too busy to ponder it. It could not bear thinking on. Like the babies, it lay there waiting for later.

Ain't got nothing, ain't got a little hand to hold. Viyella's breast ached.

And H. A.'s gone, she mourned. Not forever, though, not for good; not lost somewhere wandering around footloose in Carolina or the Southland or the whole United States, for that matter. No. H. A. was settled; he was working steady in Norfolk, Virginia. He had written and told her so. Regular. And she lived for the hour the mail truck went by, and hustled down the road each day so fast, like a wisp of paper blowing in the wind. And so many days she dragged home, her feet heavy as Shem's keg of nails, her whole body heavy, weary, hardly able to move.

The day never goes by, I don't miss H. A., she grieved. But he isn't gone for good. Never for good.

Thought I'd never get the babies off my lap.

And now her arms held emptiness.

Viyella had dizzy spells. The kitchen wheeled around her, spinning crazily, like the merry-go-round at Morehead City. Sometimes she left off stirring the soup to lie down and came back to find it a gooey mess even Jee Paw could hardly swallow. Her fried chicken was underdone. Once Jimmy cut it open and red blood ran out. He left the table in disgust. "Can't even cook no more," he grumbled. "Can't do nothing, seems, round here."

He was always grumbling, always impatient these days, so Viyella paid him no mind. But somewhere in the back of her head it lay there waiting to be thought on—when she had time. Uneasily she looked about her house. It was true there was dust on the window sill, a burned pan soaking in the sink, and dead goldenrod from summer flaking in the copper pot. The yard wasn't swept clean, and her dress, her good cotton print, had spots on it, more than Jenny Sue had ever spilled, waiting for her to wash them out.

But Viyella had terrible pains in her stomach, right up under her ribs, and thinking of Mama, she took to her bed for a spell, terrified. Elizabeth Ann began to do the cooking and to swish the broom around. She even stirred the clothes Saturdays in the old iron pot.

Ashamed, Viyella finally stumbled out.

"You have your books, sugar," she said. "You're doing so good you got to keep up. Studying. Here, I'll do it."

"Ma, just rest a bit more. Nearly done anyways." Elizabeth Ann led her gently back. "I'll get my studying in."

"Teacher says you might could get a scholarship, you work hard. Let me finish," Viyella protested. But already the pain had gripped her, doubling her over, and she gritted her teeth, unable to get more words out. Weakly, she let herself be helped back to bed.

"Don't know what's going on in there," she moaned. "Hear? Hear them noises? Sounds like a whole Yankee regiment inside." She clutched herself tensely as strange sounds, gurglings and rollings, emerged from her thin body.

"Poor Ma." Elizabeth Ann put her gentle hand down to hush the wild stomach. "Fetch you something?"

"Paregoric, maybe," said Viyella. "Costs so much, can't

hardly waste money on that. Miss Darcy Perkins takes it. Everyone knows that. Slips it from the store as calm as you please. Lives on it. No secret to no one. Elizabeth Ann? If you was to ask politely, so's not to insult her, if by chance?"

Exhausted, drawn right into a ball on the old brass bed, Viyella could say no more.

Miss Darcy Perkins gave some away from her hidden cache.

"Made me promise hope to die, not to tell," reported Elizabeth Ann. "Said it was all she had left over from her poor, dear Mama, gone so long now."

"Ha!" snorted Viyella, but she was grateful and sewed a neat seam in Miss Darcy's Irish linen handkerchief in return. And for a while she was better. But there wasn't enough to last. Not enough at all.

Watching the night fall, her hands in the sink, Viyella would sometimes forget entirely what it was she was doing, often setting the plates back without a soaping. She tried to sing:

Ev'ry night
When the sun goes in

But the words gave her no comfort; there was no solace in the blue notes. Her voice cracked and broke.

Hang my head
And lonesome cry.

"*Lonesome.*" She couldn't finish. And she couldn't cry. A prick began in the back of her eye. Harder it came, faster, until the whole side of her head felt as if Jebby Mahon were hammering on his fence posts. She lay on her bed, dishes forgotten, the scummy water still to be thrown out.

Once Thomas stood, his bewildered eyes fastened on her. She could feel them, and hastily she tried to make amends.

She hadn't heard his banjo noise and, too late, trying to laugh, she sounded more like the firecrackers on the Fourth of July.

"Get you something, Ma?" offered Jee Paw. "Cracker? Cup of water?"

She shook her head. She had neglected to praise him when he'd proudly shown her his carefully crayoned papers with the blue stars in the corner. She had meant to. She just seemed to be too busy doing. And feeling so queer all the time.

It's my age, that's what it is, she told herself. Wish Mama could tell me. My age is all. Folks with nothing to do find plenty's the matter with them, got time to ponder their heads or their stomachs.

But she pushed that thought away too. My age is all. And my arms that won't never hold a baby again. And Jenny Sue strutting along some wicked city street. And H. A. gone. My age is all, she said, and overlooked those that were at home.

So the days passed and the year. The train whistled by through the night, and the blue jays perched in the pines. Sullenly Jimmy went to work and returned, and Elizabeth Ann and Jee Paw and Thomas clung together for warmth and comfort and became their own family. Far away in Norfolk, H. A. was staying in Mrs. O. R. Johnson's steam-heated room and saving his money, sending home what he could.

Until August.

It came to be August, and now the woods and fields began to sing. And now Elizabeth Ann saw Joey Phipps down at the filling station, fell in love, and dreamed the hours away, so the soup went unstirred and the chicken burned, and all she could do was smile, her sweet, lovely smile lighting up her face and the room around her.

And now H. A.'s letters began to speak of Miss Billie Lee

Laver, of the *Virginia* Lavers. "Whatever that means," Viyella snapped scornfully to anyone who would listen, and, like Jimmy, angrily kicked a stone on her trips back from the mailbox.

And now it was almost time for school, and Thomas's teacher came to call.

And now Jimmy was laid off at the Base.

All these things happened in August, while the sweet smell of new-cut hay from Mrs. Parker's field filled the long, slumbering days and cotton clouds filled the sky.

two

"MRS. KIEFFER," said Teacher gently. "Thomas just doesn't fit in."

"Sugar, ma'am?" Viyella asked, busying herself pouring tea into her last china cup, and seeing with dismay that it was cracked. She set it down on the table and noticed, too, the splash of gravy on the oilcloth, unwiped since the night before.

"No, thank you," but Viyella bustled about anyway, fetching a spoon and the sugar bowl, her cheeks burning with shame. There was a rip in her hem so her dress hung down, ragged and uneven, and flies clustered on the stove, buzzing over bacon fat. She'd neglected to put the cotton in the screen door to keep them away. Or mop up the grease, either.

"Mrs. Kieffer," Teacher began again. "I must talk to you about Thomas."

"Is it too hot? Need cooling any?" asked Viyella anxiously, at the same time trying to tuck in the loose strands of hair straying over her face.

"It's fine, thank you. Mrs. Kieffer . . ."

Desperately, Viyella looked around for help. Any interruption would do, even Jimmy banging in or Jee Paw yelling, "Hey! Ha! Lookee! Charge, boys!" or Thomas himself running to her with a discovery. Only yesterday he'd brought a round, fuzzy caterpillar, tenderly held in the palm of his grimy little hand.

"Signifies a long, cold winter," she'd said, shaking her head grimly, and his face had fallen. So she'd tried to make amends, letting him fix a home for it in her prized copper pot, long since tarnished and barren of flowers.

But there was no distraction. The house was so still the scratching of Elizabeth Ann's pen on her Blue Horse notebook was the only sound. No help there, for sure. Elizabeth Ann spent all day in her room, dreaming and writing. Over and over, page after page was filled:

Joey Phipps
Elizabeth Ann Kieffer
love, marriage, friendship, hate, love, marriage—
Joey Phipps, I love you. Joey Phipps has the bluest eyes in the world. Joey Phipps.

Viyella hadn't needed to read it to know what was there. She could remember with a pang that turned into a pain around her heart and a breathlessness that caught her in the chest, that couldn't bear thinking about any more than Teacher's words.

"Mrs. Kieffer, please sit down," Teacher begged. "This is so important. You *must* understand."

So knowing, dreading, Viyella gave up and sat stiffly in the kitchen chair, her hands pestering her dress out of sight under the table, folding, creasing, pleating, even her shame at the appearance of her house forgotten as the words fell on her. Soft as Teacher's voice was, they were blows far worse than the back of Jimmy's hand.

"So you see, Mrs. Kieffer, we just can't be responsible."

Viyella sat quiet, only her fingers worrying the cloth. She'd always known, always expected it, ever since Thomas had first set off down the road and she had wanted to call him back.

"Mrs. Kieffer!" Teacher was becoming desperate in the face of Viyella's grim silence. She reached out for help too. "Now Elizabeth Ann. She's doing so very well, Mrs. Kieffer. I think she might win a scholarship to the University, later on, if she keeps it up. And Jee Paw. He's a smart little fellow. Very bright. You can be so proud of Jee Paw."

The words hung in the air, and at last Viyella roused herself. Her chin held high and her eyes looking directly into Teacher's, she faced her.

"I'm proud of Thomas too," she said.

"Oh yes, yes, of course." Teacher was flustered. "I didn't mean that, Mrs. Kieffer. He's a sweet little boy. Very good. But . . . but . . ."

"But he don't fit in," Viyella finished for her harshly, her eyes never wavering.

"Well, you see, he can't do what the others do. He can't understand directions, or he doesn't hear them, or . . ."

"He hears things," said Viyella. "Sometimes things no one else can hear."

"Oh yes, of course, but you see, Mrs. Kieffer," Teacher's words now tumbled about in her eagerness. "That's just it. He . . . he, the other children tease and laugh at him."

"They shouldn't ought to do that. Ain't never allowed any of mine to do that."

"No, no they shouldn't. But children don't realize, you know, and they're sometimes cruel."

"Folks is cruel." Viyella rose from the chair, her hands still, at last, at her sides.

140

Teacher rose too, reaching for her patent leather pocket-book and smoothing her skirt in one motion. "It would be kinder to keep him at home, Mrs. Kieffer."

"It would hurt his feelings not to go off with the others," said Viyella. "And with his father t'home now, ain't right for him to be here. Maybe if H. A. were here to teach him . . ." She sighed and Teacher misunderstood.

"I knew you'd be sensible. It *is* hard, I know, but in the long run . . ."

"Why can't you make a place for him, if he can't do it by himself?" Viyella's voice was as cold as her eyes.

"I have so many to tend, Mrs. Kieffer, so much to . . ."

"Always room for one more. Got to be, most times. And Thomas can make things, you know," she said eagerly, persuasively. "Out of wood, bark, twigs, even. And he can paint pictures. And the songs he can whistle! Sometimes I think it's the mourning dove outside the window, and it's Thomas instead, right at my elbow."

Viyella smiled, and Teacher, confused, smiled back.

"But that's just it, you see," she said. "That's why . . ."

"You can help make him a place, ma'am, can't you?" Viyella didn't plead; it was a statement. "You try him some more, this year. Jee Paw's near about big enough to take care of those kids that plague him. Just about," she mused.

"Mrs. Kieffer," Teacher began again, and then sur-rendered. Hastily she went to the door, barely remembering to say, "Nice meeting you. Thank you for the tea."

Untouched, the tea had cooled in its cracked cup, as cold now as Viyella's voice. "Nice to meet you too, ma'am. Come sit again."

Viyella hardly waited for the door to shut before she ran and fetched cotton. Then she flicked at the flies with her rolled-up apron and squashed them in the bacon grease be-fore carrying the whole mess out and stuffing it under the blackberry bush. Scraping the gravy with a knife, she mopped it up and then, seating herself in the rocker, she sewed up the hem in her dress, even while it was on her.

"Elizabeth Ann," she called. "Elizabeth Ann, come out here!" finally hollering when there was no response.

"You mind the house, hear?" she said when at last her daughter emerged. "Have Thomas fetch some greens, Queen Anne's lace, what he can find. We'll stick them in the Coke bottle for now. Can't imagine how this house got this way! Sweep up, too, sugar," she added more gently. "I'm going on over to the Base to see what I can do. Wash clothes, maybe, for the wives, or sew them up something. Cook up some chicken real good too, please, if I ain't back. Just don't put Joey Phipps in the pot!" Viyella laughed.

"Oh, Ma," Elizabeth Ann laughed too. Then, sobering, "You up to it? How you going to get there and back? You ain't strong enough to . . ."

"I'm strong enough," said Viyella.

Got to eat, don't we? she continued to herself. Thomas got to go to school, too, for now anyways, till I can ponder what to do with him. Got to put redbud, honeysuckle, holly in the copper pot, too, as comes time. Soon's the caterpillar moves on out, it's going to get such a polishing it never had to pleasure the eye, she vowed. H. A.'s gone, but the world can't stop just for that. There's the others.

And what if H. A. came home and found her dress spotted and her hair uncombed and the bed still holding the shape of Jimmy long past midday? And what if he brought Miss Billie Lee Laver, of the Virginia Lavers, with him?

Don't like the sound of that girl, Viyella mumbled to herself. Not at all I don't. What is she doing with H. A.? Her with her fancy ways? What does she know about washing his shirts just so for him, stewing the chicken, mending his jeans? What does she know about getting up in the night to tend a sick one, herself too tired to move? What does she know about going to bed hungry and cold sometimes, and wearing an old cotton dress? Couldn't know nothing about any of that, waited on hand and foot in her big house in all her finery. And how can H. A. measure up to all that? Isn't right. What is she doing to H. A.?

But then Viyella had to be fair in spite of herself. It wasn't fitting for a boy to send so much home to keep his family, either. It was only right he'd want to store some by for his own life. And hadn't she urged him to escape while he could? To save himself? But that didn't mean Miss Billie Lee Laver too.

When the letter came, Viyella put every pot in the house on to boil furiously. She scoured the stove and got down on her knees and went over the worn linoleum with a scrub brush. She looked in the copper pot, but the caterpillar was still living there, and she was sorry. What a shining she'd have given it! Miss Billie Lee Laver!

"Dear Ma," wrote H. A. "I'm sorry I can't send so much home no more, but I know you will be glad of the reason. I'm saving up so Billie Lee and I can get married. I know you would like her and love her same as me."

"Huh!" snorted Viyella.

"And I hope to bring her on home sometime. She is so pretty and sweet and so little I can hold all of her in my two hands."

Better watch that, H. A., warned Viyella across the long miles north to Norfolk, Virginia.

"Her folks don't care for me and I don't care for them neither, but it don't matter to Billie Lee. Anyways aim to show them I can take care of her good.

"So I hope you don't miss the money too much. If you need it I'll send it on and figure some other way."

Need it! But Viyella could never ask, never play that

trick, undermining H. A. with his girl. Even if it was true.
"Hope this finds you well.

Your son
H. A.

Jee Paw getting big?"

Yes, sir, he is, answered Viyella, banging pots, and a lucky thing too. Thank the good Lord and certainly not you, H. A. He's big enough to protect Thomas. Almost. Big enough anyways to run errands for Shem, tote things around the community for folks. Gets some nickels and dimes that way, filling up the coffee can, and it all adds up, keeps us going.

And there was another lucky thing, now nothing else was coming in. The wives at the Base didn't need washing done; the colored women saw to that. But they admired the seams Viyella sewed, and word got around from one to the other. Now women drove over for Viyella's nimble, swift fingers to hem their skirts and darn their table linen. Such things as they had! Viyella shook her head in wonder. Didn't seem to even notice them, either; took them for granted, probably like Miss Billie Lee in all her finery!

Once or twice Jimmy had mumbled about seeking work somewhere else, and Viyella thought, Off again. Chasing Emerald? Will he come back this time? But the terrible fear and panic and dread of the past were gone, and she felt only numbness. The truth was, it was only talk. Jimmy was too dispirited to move on right now. Wasn't any work nowheres anyway, or so Jebby said. Now Jimmy stood outside, leaning on his car, a heap of rusted, twisted ruins in the yard, junk to be sold, but when she suggested it, his eyes flashed. He clung to the remains.

"You crazy, woman?" he yelled angrily. "Sell my car?"

"We need the money, Jimmy," Viyella began softly, then had the sense to hold her tongue.

"Good times come, I'll fix her up again. You'll see."

144

A week or so later another letter came, and Viyella's heart flip-flopped like the catfish Jee Paw brought in to eat. For a minute she gripped her breast, afraid of all the old ailments, and God Amighty, she thought, what will I do if they come on back? But then she smiled tenderly, remembering.

Dear Ma,

We're married, Billie Lee and me. We run away but now we're back and we got a license and Mrs. Johnson is letting her stay in my room for just a little extra. Her folks pass us by on the street but she don't care. She's looking for work but I won't let her. She ain't too strong, she's so little. You would love her as I do. I'll bring her home when I can.

H. A.

Tell Jee Paw hello. Thomas and Elizabeth Ann too. from H. A.

Kind of sudden, wasn't it, H. A.? thought Viyella. Up and running off like that? But I would love her, she admitted. Yes, H. A., I would, poor little thing, puny and frail and having to move off from her folks because of you. And living in your room, steam-heated or no, when she's used to a big, fine house. And looking for work to help you, when what in God's creation could she work at? She must love you mightily to do all that for you, H. A. And make you happy. So I do, too, love her. Poor little thing.

Elizabeth Ann was so excited at the news she forgot to stay in her room.

"H. A. married," she breathed, "H. A. married!" and Viyella knew what thoughts were in her head. She and Joey Phipps in a steam-heated room.

Thomas was baffled. "Billie Lee?" he asked. "Billie Lee?"

"Like a new sister," explained Jee Paw. Oh, how he stuck

out his chest now. H. A., his brother, had a wife.

Viyella was late with Mrs. McCutcheon's coat because she sat fashioning a blouse of the finest lace she could buy at the Economy for Billie Lee. She took the money from her hidden store in the coffee can.

"Don't care if I do use it," she said. "We can eat a little less, won't hurt none, and I can patch up Jee Paw's jeans once again. My daughter-in-law should have a pretty wedding dress."

She cut it from Elizabeth Ann, figuring if Billie Lee was so small, it should fit, and mailed it off to Norfolk, proudly addressed to Mrs. H. A. Kieffer.

It did fit and Billie Lee liked it and wore it "special for H. A." She wrote and said so and "thank you very much."

Viyella was happy thinking of them. But the caterpillar stayed huddled up in a round, fuzzy, little black ball in the copper pot, searching for warmth, and the long months were upon them, the short, dark days, turning quickly to night.

three

DREARY, DREARY was the winter, the skies gray, overcast always like Viyella's spirit, and cold. It seemed as if she could never be warm again, high as Jee Paw built the fire. Folks talked of nothing else, that and the layoffs at the Base, as, chilled and shivering even under layers of thin sweaters, they met at Shem's or the Economy.

Jimmy talked of neither. He stayed home most of the time, and along about February he began to cough from sitting by the cold fire without stirring the coals, just waiting for Jee Paw to come home and build it up. Or maybe it was

146

from wandering around in the yard with icy winds blowing and dampness from the sea soaking his chest as he poked the remains of his car, twiddling the door handle and brushing blown oak leaves and pine needles off the peeling hood. Or maybe from coming home from the Bucket in the raw night air, his coat forgotten, and taking extra time for his feet to find the road.

The cough turned violent, racking his body, doubling him, and when he retched into the kitchen sink, along with whatever bits and pieces of food he'd managed to swallow came thick black sputum. Soon he wasn't eating at all. Viyella spent her carefully hoarded money for succulent ham. She simmered chicken in herbs till the meat fell off the bones in tenderness and made hoecake every night. But Jimmy only nibbled, pushed his chair back, and left the table to stand by the window, staring out into the blackness, watching for Jenny Sue to come back, or for a light down by the highway in Emerald's house that would mean she was there again, or even for H. A.'s tall lean figure heading home. Then his shoulders pressed forward, his chest caved in, and the panicky, frustrated noises of his body protesting would begin. He'd rest his forehead against the cool of the glass, trying to catch his breath, soothe his burning face, keep his foothold. He became as thin and rib-ridged as Viyella, and one night his legs doubled up beneath him. His hands flailed wildly, then caught a brief grip on the window sill, and Jee Paw ran to him, clutching him by the belt flapping in his jeans.

His fall was broken and he was only bruised, but as he lay on the old linoleum floor his blue eyes stared unseeing at the unfinished, rough ceiling, and his breathing seemed a presence in the room. When Viyella put her hand to his cheek, she drew it back as quickly as if she'd touched hot bacon grease spattering on the stove.

She called Elizabeth Ann and even Thomas, but Jimmy

was so frail that she and Jee Paw could easily have managed to carry him to the old iron bed.

Then began the days and nights, each blending into the other, that were broken only by the scuffling of the children going off to school, Elizabeth Ann's soft voice, the return of Thomas with leaves and mud and bark to make a poultice for Jimmy's rigid throat, and Shem Baker coming once with a bag of ice to sponge him off.

The dismal days got worse. No remedy sufficed. And it was all from the listlessness, the dead fire, the ruined heap on the bare spot in the yard, the long, endless footsteps trying to find the way home on the sandy, rutted road.

So was this the end? Viyella sorrowed, mopping Jimmy's wet face with the old checkered handkerchief, already drenched with his sweat. Is this the end of the road for you, Jimmy?

"Elizabeth Ann." She called softly, so as not to wake him. But poor Jimmy, what could he hear where he was, anyway, she wondered, except voices unknown to her, sounds humming in his ears, noises banging relentlessly in his throbbing head? "Fetch another cloth and wring this out, hon. Be spry."

But there was no need to add that. Elizabeth Ann was already at his bed, so silent Viyella hadn't heard her over the heavy clutching for breath, the harsh rasp that filled the room even as Jimmy heaved under the quilts.

"I'll sit a minute, Ma," Elizabeth Ann offered, "to spell you. You been here so long and never touched your soup, neither."

"Thank you, sweetheart." Viyella didn't take her eyes from Jimmy, but she knew how Elizabeth Ann looked standing there in her clean, cotton dress, not a spill on it like Jenny Sue's had always had, her fair hair pulled back out of the way, shining clean, too, and her eyes gentle. I am blessed even so, thought Viyella, wanting to fold her arms around her and kiss the soft cheek. But her hands were busy holding the quilts around Jimmy's neck, keeping him warm.

"You're tired too," she said, "keeping the house and the kids. And you nursed him last night, sugar, so good."

Elizabeth Ann had, too. It wasn't just stick dolls to make well this time, but all the hours of practice had made her soothing and deft, and when Jimmy had suddenly sat bolt upright and cried out in terror words and things she shouldn't know, her face had been calm and sad only, as she pressed him lightly back into the pillow.

"Done more than your part," Viyella barely murmured, but Elizabeth Ann heard her as she came back with a clean dry rag and, bending over Jimmy, gently mopped the moisture from her father's forehead.

"Here, Ma." She handed the rag to Viyella. "If you need me, I'll be in the kitchen waiting on the boys."

She smiled briefly and Viyella nodded.

"Thank you," she said again helplessly. "I figure to stay by him now, darlin'. Might want you later for company."

Or . . . but her mind ran away from that. "Oh, Lord, not Jimmy," she started fervently, but her heart ran away from that too. She couldn't pray, couldn't weep, couldn't do anything but sit there; the words and feelings choked in her throat like the phlegm in Jimmy's chest. *God Amighty, not Jimmy*, she prayed.

Not Jimmy, she pleaded, remembering his lively blue eyes so clear, like the sky over the water tower that day as the wind blew his shirttail and ruffled his black hair, dark as the shadows in the swamp, when he saw clear to Charlotte. Not laughing, swaggering, bragging Jimmy setting out to see the world and enjoying every sight, pleasuring himself so with a smack of the lips at a taste of beer, a grin at a pretty girl. Oh, yes. That too. But so alive.

And now he lay, burning and choking, ending up in the old brass bed under Viyella's worn quilts.

It didn't seem right somehow, she thought. He hadn't fallen off that tower, even when his foot missed a rung. The Rockfish and Aberdeen hadn't smashed him when he danced along the tracks ahead of the Cannonball. Shem Baker hadn't left a mark, the time they had the fight over the hound dog. And he had never lain in the ditch, either, all the times he was coming home late in the dark of the moon. Not Jimmy.

"All the times I could have touched you, turned to you," she whispered, "but there was H. A. or Thomas or Fella or the pot boiling over on the stove. Figure to stay right here with you now, Jimmy. Want to stay here, Jimmy." She kissed his eyelids where they lay closed over the bright blue eyes. "What I wish is I'd laughed at your jokes or danced with you close at the Bucket or sung you a happy tune, instead of all the time grieving and pondering. Wish I'd shown you the sun glinting on the pine needles so shiny. Wish I could have felt it warm on my back, alongside you. Wish you could have seen my cardinal flashing in the chinaberry tree. Wish I could cry, Jimmy."

She laid her head down and buried it in the hollow of his neck. The stubble of his beard pricked her face, sharp, so it hurt, and she was glad.

"Remember the times you grinned and called me 'sugar'? Times you stroked my hair, times I lay in your arms, times you made faces at Fella and listened to Thomas's tuba noises? Times you brought Jenny Sue her dresses, so happy and proud you was? And now there's your car, bent and ruined, just a heap, and us like it," Viyella mourned. "Always thought it'd be me; ailing all the time I was, birthing and such, and you with never even a runny nose like Elizabeth Ann. So strong you was. And now . . ."

His chest heaved again, and the sounds in his throat were ghastly. Her head flew up and she screamed in terror, but when Elizabeth Ann got to the bed, Viyella was still. Her hand, both hands, reached under the quilts and gripped his, hard, as she clenched her fingers, tightly holding on to him.

"Hold on now. Hold on. *Live!*" she cried, her voice breaking.

Elizabeth Ann picked up the forgotten cloth and began to wipe his face, but Viyella yelled, "No! Leave him be."

"There's so much left still, Jimmy," she promised him. "You'll see. Jenny Sue might come on home just the same. And Elizabeth Ann, so sweet, so kind; you'd love her too, Jimmy, do already, only you don't know it, mixed up as you are in your mind. The boys'll want you to teach them to shoot, know that? Well, maybe not Thomas, but he can watch, long's you just hit tin cans and things. And they all down at the Bucket want to hear you sing 'Candy.' I want to hear you sing 'Candy,' and the sound of your foot on the orange crate. Did you ever know what a comforting noise that was to me? How I listened for it? Then the night was right, the world was right again, like the train going through, your foot scraping outside. Jimmy was home.

"Can't take back the years, Jimmy. That's the true sorrow, ain't it? All the deeds done and words said, and I'd give my soul to do it again. Give my soul and my copper pot thrown in too, to do different. Oh, to take it all back and commence again. Of all the years, save only the good ones.

"Jimmy," she begged.

Thomas and Jee Paw huddled in the doorway, and Elizabeth Ann stood motionless behind her, but Viyella didn't see them. She hardly saw Jimmy either, his face a blur of all the days and all the years, happy, and angry . . . alive.

"Jimmy! C'mon!" Now she shouted, and her fingers held his in a vise.

Darkness came with the sound of the train going by down below across the fields, and still Viyella sat, her hands frozen now around his, looking down at his pale, thin face. His eyebrows drawn together in pain, his mouth working, a muscle in his cheek twitching, his knees thrashing, his body fought the quilts and the unknown. Jimmy was restless even now. Now more than ever.

Torn apart again, she thought, between going and staying. Not like you, Jimmy, fearing what's ahead. But do you know somehow, you aren't done with what's behind? It was always so for you, wasn't it, poor Jimmy? Always torn apart between going and staying?

"Jimmy, don't go off again. Not now," she pleaded, as she had so many times before, the words sounding as useless, as futile as they had then. So she gripped the harder.

The house was hushed and quiet; only small sounds came from the kitchen: the clink of a spoon against the tin pot, the thump of fresh logs Jee Paw brought for the fire, the "shhh" for Thomas and his answering "shhh."

The door was slightly ajar, and the faint light coming through gleamed on the iron bedstead. What a heap of living this bed has held, Viyella thought. And dying, she added grimly. For a brief minute, the image of the bed dismantled, the mattress tied to the top of Jimmy's car, came into her mind. A sorry sight, heading where? she wondered. Folks not even noticing as it went by, unless it was to laugh, never knowing the stories the old brass could tell, every lump in that mattress accounted for. Never caring, either.

In the midst of her grief and fear, the sadness of it overwhelmed Viyella, and she saw the bedstead, as rusty as Jimmy's car, lying useless, as the auctioneer's gavel banged down, no one ever knowing or caring that once Viyella and Jimmy had lain there, and Grandpa before them; the babies born, the sickness tended, the bodies dying.

So what was the use? What was it all for? It meant nothing in the end, nothing more than an old hubcap rolled alongside the highway: the soggy ticking mixed with the wet leaves of February, the bedpost tarnished and thrown in the dump. It would be like a forgotten gravestone in the rain, grass choking it, pushing it to one side, to live itself. Was that it? Was that what it was all about?

All forgotten, yes, or never known. No account, none of it. Oh, but someone should know, should care! She gripped Jimmy's hands with her fingers, numb but warm.

His hands limp in her own, his body spent, Jimmy lay still. She could hardly hear his breathing and barely see the faint rise and fall of his chest.

"Jimmy," she moaned.

His eyes opened, and the kitchen light pinpointed his pupils, so for a minute it was as if they were blue as ever, piercing her.

"Vi," he said clearly, and smiled.

"Jimmy."

"Vi," he repeated. "Prettiest little angel," and he was off again, mumbling. Who knew where his mind was? Back in the Christmas Pageant where she had knelt over the baby? Dreaming, confused, gone where she could not follow him. But he had known her.

It was close to dawn. She could hear the birds rustling, getting ready for the day, and back of the dark wall of pines a lightness began, touching only the tops, but spreading. The fresh, pungent smell of early morning came through the cracks around the window.

Got to have Jee Paw stuff them up again, thought Viyella absently. Send him to fetch some newspapers from Shem today. Draft's bad for Jimmy.

"Well, Jimmy. Oh, Jimmy," she cried, but softly, so as not to disturb him. There he lay, his eyes closed in deep sleep, his forehead cool at last, breathing evenly but with a scraping sound, like his shoe on the orange crate.

It took her some time to unloose her fingers from his, so still they were and cramped. Rigid, inflexible, they curved around an unseen hand. And it was a long time after that be-

153

fore she could bend them, and then, as life and feeling returned, they were filled with pain.

Jimmy's strength did not come back easily. It was days before he could sit up in bed for any length of time while Viyella patiently spooned, urged, coaxed broth between his dry lips. And days more before he could swing around with the help of Jee Paw so his legs hung over the side of the bed. More than a week went by before he could walk, and even then he leaned heavily on Viyella and Elizabeth Ann and stopped every few steps to rest, panting with fatigue. Whiskey helped, but it was dangerous, inspiring false courage and well-being that led afterward to desperate exhaustion.

Sometimes he would sit by the fire, which Jee Paw now heaped up in the morning as well as after school, and stare out the window, seeing nothing; but he spent most of his time in bed, tossing aimlessly both day and night, his eyes closed in restless sleep or darting from side to side, glancing off the familiar iron bedpost, the nail on the wall with his shirt and jeans hanging down from it, or the quilts piled high in readiness at the foot of his bed.

He was weak, and everything irritated him; even the soft sound of the pines swishing against the window made him nervous.

"Vi," he would call, as if she could stop the wind. And when she came running, he'd scowl and complain about it being too hot in the room, or too cold, and why hadn't Jee Paw fixed the cracks?

"He did, Jimmy, just yesterday. Stuffed them real good." She pointed it out to him, but already he was complaining about his shirt being prickly . . . she'd put in too much starch again.

She'd fallen behind in her sewing and had to sit up late at night; and then, often as not, she'd have to drop it in her chair to run in at the sound of Jimmy's fretful voice.

154

Tired herself from scurrying to and fro trying to keep the children quiet and Jimmy at peace, it was all she could do not to snap back at him.

"I wished him well. Begged, pleaded, willed it, prayed, promised my copper pot, too," she reminded herself as Jimmy called for something else.

"Hush, children, quiet. Daddy's trying to sleep so he can get better," she shushed them, but it was getting harder to do. Finding fault and bickering were catching, and they could spread through a house faster than gnat bugs in April. Thomas was bewildered; Jee Paw was getting downright cross and assertive. Oh, how like H. A. he looked, Viyella thought, standing his ground, his feet spread apart for confidence and balance, the ridiculous cowlick pointing straight toward the ceiling. Even gentle Elizabeth Ann was becoming impatient.

Why was it? Viyella wondered. Why can't you hang on to the big things, the beautiful times, the moments with meaning shining right through? The giving, the love? Why does it always come down to "Soup's too hot" or "Stew's got too much pepper"?

Desperately she tried to remember when Jimmy had opened his eyes and whispered "Vi" and had known her and all that was and might have been. But all she heard was the whine of his voice complaining; all she saw was the blankness of his face gazing past her.

So the dismal, dreary days of winter passed on into March. Jimmy's feet steadied themselves enough now to lurch to the Bucket on a Saturday night. It seemed as if Jee Paw grew another inch, and Elizabeth Ann was all blushes and giggles again, scribbling in her Blue Horse notebook. The swamp lightened for Thomas to explore. The nights became shorter and dusk longer (bit by bit, not so you'd notice it all at once) for Viyella to do her sewing by and for Jimmy to stare out at the wall of pines. But there was a stirring in the branches, a rustling in the needles, a promise of spring, of life, of beginning again.

four

THERE WAS no warning, not a sound, not even steps scuffling on the sand or the scrape of a foot on the orange crate. Too long Viyella had listened, and now she didn't hear.

By the last light of day, she sat bent over Mrs. Hollis McAvoy's black velveteen, carefully setting in the lace collar where it had been carelessly ripped at the Saturday night officers' party. Jimmy lay in bed, half awake, half asleep, in the only rest he knew these days. Jee Paw had gone off on one of Shem Baker's errands; Elizabeth Ann was shut in her room writing "Joey Phipps" in her Blue Horse notebook; Thomas was down in the fields where he went, safely now, to watch the lonely train come through before dark. So Viyella was alone and had no warning.

The door opened and creaked shut, and still she bent over her needle, frowning, her eyes not so sharp as they once had been.

"That you, Jee Paw? Sure was a quick one." When there was no answer, she said, "Thomas? I didn't hear the train come on. You tired of watching?" With still no answer, she looked up.

It was spring and the redbud had burst into bloom when H. A. brought his baby home.

He stood there tall, still thin in his manhood, his cheek bones high, so like Viyella's own, shadows below them. His hair was darker now, and his deep brown eyes were circled in sadness. A kerchief stuffed with belongings was slung over his shoulder, and in his arms he carried a bundle wrapped in a ragged blue blanket.

One shoe was held together by string, and the other had a great gaping hole along the side. And in a dream, before she even thought, Viyella sighed, "Oh, H. A., you and your shoes." And then she cried, "H. A.!" jumping up, black velveteen and lace falling unheeded from her lap. But, beginning to run toward him, she stopped, suddenly shy, and reached back, her hand gripping the arm of her rocker for strength. "H. A.," she whispered.

He stood hesitant too, as if unsure that he would be welcome or that this was his home. He saw that the burlap curtains were gone, frayed beyond repair, and in their place hung a sad, jaunty calico print, Mrs. H. Roy Taintor's old gardening dress remade. And the linoleum was worn thin, down to the bare floorboard, where he knew Viyella stood at the kitchen sink in the evenings, her hands in dishwater, her eyes off in the dark ring of pines, and her heart far away. But there was the copper teakettle, filled now with forsythia, and there was the rocking chair newly nailed together and freshly painted green over old scars. And there was his mother.

H. A. stood a minute, his eyes resting on her. "Ma," he said. Then going to her, "Hey, Ma." He grinned, holding out his bundle. "Brought you something, Ma."

For a terrible moment she stood quiet, holding back, terrified to hold the small burden in her arms, afraid to uncover the blanket, fear and dread striking her still as she remembered another spring, another day, another baby.

"Ma," H. A. said gently. "Sit down now, Ma, and I'll put him in your lap." He pushed her lightly and settled the baby in her arms. He pulled back the blanket slowly, and she couldn't believe how small the little body was. The knees were bent, and showing just under the little fat belly were the legs, the feet. Long and slim like his father's.

"Oh Lordy, he's got your feet, H. A.!" She took her head, clucking to herself, laughing and crying within.

A small round arm came up and clasped its hand on her shoulder. The other hand reached out, and tiny fingers pressed tightly into her arm.

Viyella rubbed her cheek on the dark fuzz of hair and saw with blurred eyes the heartbeat with a life of its own in the soft spot. She felt a hand on her head, light, comforting, and a quick brush of lips against her face; then H. A. was tucking the blanket in carefully around his baby, and Viyella's tears stained it along with the grime and dust of the trip.

I'm crying, she thought wonderingly, I'm crying. Not a tear left in me and now such a rushing.

To feel the warmth, the softness, the stout, trusting beat of the heart, the little chest against her own. To hold a baby in her arms again.

"Dark in here, Ma, you know that?" H. A. flicked the light and set his kerchief on the kitchen table. "He'll be tuning up directly, Ma. Got to get his vittles like any other folks."

But Viyella couldn't look up from the baby's head, matted now, and wet. She couldn't free a hand to wipe her eyes, either, for all the good it would do.

"He's gonna have brown eyes, too, know it?" H. A. bustled about, heating water on the stove and setting a bottle in it. "You'll see them, soon enough."

"Hey! Elizabeth Ann!" and as she stood shyly in the doorway, he went to her. "Don't you know me? I'm H. A. home again." He held out a leg and wiggled his torn shoe. "Don't you recall my big feet?"

For an awful second he was afraid, but his mother rocked on, heedless, and he tickled Elizabeth Ann till she giggled. "Grown mighty pretty, I'd say," and she blushed amidst the giggles. "Boys buzzing round like bees on the honey-suckle, hey?"

"Oh, H. A.!" She ducked her head and looked up at him through long lashes in a gesture so like Jenny Sue's that his heart caught. But her smile was soft and bashful.

"Thomas!" H. A. was grabbed by the tough lean calf of his leg and hung on to, and Thomas laughed and blew out his cheeks in his tuba noise, clinging the harder the more H. A. tried to dislodge him. "Hey there, the water's boiling over!" Dragging Thomas along with him, H. A. strode to the stove, aware all the time of a skinny, bony, awkward little boy, with a paintbrush of hair sticking up at the back of his head, standing in the doorway. H. A. put the bottle on the table and turning back said, "Hey, Jee Paw, give me a hand here, will you? No darn good at these things."

Together they struggled with the nipple and then stood apart. "Hey, Jee Paw. How you?"

Jee Paw nodded his head.

"Growed a foot, ain't you?" H. A. ruffled the back of the cowlick and dropped his hand on Jee Paw's shoulder.

Then there was a gasping breath, and another, as the baby's chest heaved and a wonderful, lusty wail came from his furious little red face. He gathered forces and let out another.

Thomas looked startled, Elizabeth Ann came closer, Jee Paw and H. A. both grabbed for the bottle, and Viyella began to laugh.

"Hurry up," she scolded. "Mind now. Not too hot. Hurry up! Little fella's hungry."

Jimmy heard the racket and roused himself from bed. He sat a minute, shaking his head, tentatively scratching at his undershirt, then slowly made his way to the kitchen. There rocked Viyella, crooning, a lump of blue blanket in her arms, and there were his children, all talking at once, clustered around the long legs of his oldest son.

"Come home, I see," said Jimmy, and now there was instant silence in the room; even Viyella hushed as she clutched the baby more fiercely in her arms. "Couldn't get along on your own? Wasn't the man you thought you was, eh?"

"I got along," said H. A., waiting.

"Aim to stay?" Jimmy headed for the window ledge and his cigars.

"Got a lot of plans to talk about," H. A. answered. "If you're willing."

"Whatcha got there?" he gestured toward Viyella with his cigar.

"My son." H. A. never took his eyes from his father's face. "Born about a month ago. Wrote you and Ma about it."

"Well, what do you know?" Jimmy's voice softened, and he started forward to inspect the baby. "Think of that," he mused admiringly, and grinned. "What's his name?"

"Woodrow Redfern Kieffer," announced H. A. proudly.

Jimmy stopped. He stood absolutely still, breathing heavily, his pale, sickly face suffused with red and stifled anger.

"That there a briarpatch child?" he roared.

"Jimmy! That's your grandson!" Viyella cried as H. A. winced, his face filled with pain.

"Well is he or ain't he? You skulking home to hide him? Where's his ma?" Viciously Jimmy tore off the end of his cigar and spat the plug at H. A.'s feet.

"His ma is dead," said H. A., his voice rough and uneven, but deep now, with no more frog croaks, no boy shrillness. "And she was my wife. Legal. Billie Lee Laver Kieffer. My wife."

Jimmy chewed a minute longer, glaring fiercely at his son, but he was tiring. He sank down on the hearthstone, his shoulders slumping. His voice had lost its sureness.

"Why ain't he with her folks?" he tried belligerently.

"Why bring him here, make more work on all of us? Why don't they want him if it's legal? Eh?"

"Because I'm his father," said H. A. "Aim to raise my son my way, not theirs, with their fancy tricks and silly airs. Aim to raise my son on his own land, too."

"You mean you aim to have your ma raise him, now your pretty Miss Billie Lee is gone?"

H. A.'s face flickered with pain again, but he repeated, "He's *my* son. I aim to raise him."

The baby had fallen asleep, nestled in Viyella's arms, his head drooping against her breast. H. A. took away the bottle and then gently removed the small body.

"We'll talk of it later, Pa. This little fella's worn out." H. A. carried him against his shoulder, one large hand awkwardly, tenderly, holding his head, the other bracing the round little bottom.

"Hey, Ma." He turned and grinned. "Ain't much use at this. He's soaked all the way through."

Viyella jumped up and rummaged in the kerchief. Her old cotton was soaked through, too, but she never noticed or knew whether from the baby or her tears or a mixture of both.

"First thing to do tomorrow is to fix him up decent," she said.

Long after, far into the night, with the house asleep and the fire dying low in the fireplace, Viyella rocked the baby and pondered on other things.

"What I aim to do," explained H. A. seriously as they sat at the table, supper over, the plates gone cold with redeye gravy unheeded before them, "is go on back home, Ma. Plant, farm, pay up the back taxes taken out of the crops . . ."

Thomas was still, his eyes solemn, and even Elizabeth Ann held her place, not disappearing to the privacy of her room and notebook, while H. A. continued. "Take a lot of work to fix up Grampa's farm. Weeds, brush all over, I know, but it's good soil, rich underneath. Don't care for cities, Ma; always did want to work the earth. And I'm strong. Might even get some help too, hey, Jee Paw? Looks to me like you fixed the rocker pretty good."

Jee Paw grinned and nodded his head vigorously, his eyes bright with anticipation.

"Can run errands for Vinny, too, maybe." Then, not forgetting Thomas, H. A. turned to the grave little boy. "Hey, Thomas, there's a place there where the woods meet the fields, higher than here. You can see mountains far off, and the birds come if you're still."

"Cardinals? Are there cardinals?" Thomas asked.

"Lots of cardinals. Sunflower seed they like and we'll get it, put it out for them, and you can help me too, can't you? Wasn't it you painted Ma's rocker so fresh? We'll have a lot of painting to do."

"You sure as hell will," said Jimmy. "Place will have fallen down around its stilts by now. Damndest idea I ever heard." He sat hunched over, twiddling the mess on his plate with his fork. Now he let it fall, clinking on the tin, and stood up.

"Was a solid house, Pa, just take some time to fix."

"And where will Jee Paw and Thomas be living while you fix it? Eh? Rain pouring through the roof, wind blowing in the cracks. Eh? And what about your ma, think of that? What she gonna do without her boys? Just mind yours?"

He dug his thumbs in his jeans and balanced his weight on the back of his heels, confident of scoring a point.

"Figured it this way, Pa," said H. A. "I'd go on ahead and get the house set, maybe get seed put in. Not too late, reckon. Send for y'all later, after school lets out."

"Send for us later!" Jimmy shouted. "God-damn-it-to-hell-sweet-Jesus! Who you think you are!"

162

"It's an idea, Pa; wanted to talk it over."

"And your Ma watches your little 'un while you do this?"

"Would you mind, Ma?"

Viyella couldn't answer.

"Wouldn't be too long, month or so. Thought Jee Paw, the kids, would want to finish up the year at school before they went."

Now there was a strangled sound, and Elizabeth Ann darted from her chair and into her hiding place.

Joey Phipps, thought Viyella. Wouldn't, couldn't bear to leave Joey Phipps.

But there were Thomas and Jee Paw, hanging on to their brother, afire with excitement. And there was H. A.'s brown-eyed baby asleep on her quilts. And there was the memory of a ridge of blue, far off, mingling with the smoke haze, the pines, and the pungent smell of the fire in autumn. And there was Elizabeth Ann in her room, sobbing into her notebook.

I should go to her, Viyella thought, and comfort her. Maybe sometime later when it's settled, one way or the other, I will. But there was no comfort against loss, against knowing the fear of loss.

"Ma?" H. A. leaned toward her anxiously. "When you get there, I can do a lot for him. I know how, I guess." He tried a grin. "You won't have to do it alone."

Won't have to do it alone. Viyella bent her head. How could she bear it all again? The hunger, the hurting, the loving. The clasping fingers, the heavy, sleepy head on her breast.

"I'm too weary to raise another," she sighed, not looking at him. And what of Jimmy? she thought.

"Ma." H. A. touched her chin to lift it, to see her face, but he stopped midway and left her in peace. Jee Paw and Thomas set up a clamor, tugging at her skirts, and Jimmy's laughter drowned out the aching sounds through the wall.

"Big idea, H. A.," he said. "Big idea. What did you think was to become of Ma's sewing? Eh? Makes some nice cash out of that. Can't do that and raise a young'un."

"There's the Exchange there," said H. A. "Takes things and Yankee ladies buys them. Anyways, I'm going to look after Woody too. Told you that. And he won't be a baby for long."

"Don't care so much for sewing," Viyella mumbled to herself. "Never did, and my eyes bothers me some now."

But no one heard because they were all talking at once. Jimmy's voice was loudest.

"And me? What am I supposed to do, eh? Young punk coming home telling his own Pa what's what. Me? How about me?"

What could he say? H. A. wondered. What did Jimmy do now anyways? It would only rouse him more to mention it. But H. A. knew, they all must know, that it was the scrapings, the bits and pieces of change from the errands, the sewing, the sitting, that kept the family tied together, like old parts of frayed string, knotted here and there for strength where it could be.

"Heard they was laying folks off at the Base," he said gently, to spare Jimmy, pretend. "Thought there might be something back there. I'd need a hand in the fields."

Jimmy was speechless with anger. His narrowed eyes and contorted face frightened Viyella. She went to him, but he shook her off.

"No planting, plowing for me!" he yelled. "God damn it, no!"

He stalked to the door and slammed it on his way out, and then, through the sudden silence, Elizabeth Ann's anguished weeping seemed to fill the room.

"Sorry, Ma." Now H. A. slumped, his head bowed. "Seemed like a good idea. Sorry."

164

"Was a good idea," said Viyella as she went to Elizabeth Ann's door. "Was a fine idea, H. A., if things could all fit together."

"Just riled him, upset the whole lot of you." H. A. covered his eyes with his hand.

Torn apart, forever torn apart, thought Viyella, her hand on the door knob. And now, how do I go in and tell Elizabeth Ann there'll be other boys, other years, other names to write in the Blue Horse notebook? How do I tell her there'll be another Joey Phipps when there won't and may never be? Ever.

The baby was howling, but when Viyella got there, H. A. had already balanced him against his shoulder with one hand and with the other turned on the faucet to fill a pan with water.

"Here, I'll take him," said Viyella. "Hush now, hush," she soothed. "Ain't as bad as all that." She carried the baby to the rocker and settled herself. "Hurry up, H. A., he's mad!"

H. A. brought the bottle, and with a quick turn of his head the baby caught the nipple in his mouth and began to gulp lustily. He fixed his father with a watchful, dark eye as he went about his business.

H. A. grinned down at him. "Sure is a strong little fella," he said proudly.

"Round my shoulders some more, toting him," said Viyella.

"Ma?"

"I'm too tired to raise another, H. A. Ain't fitting anyways for a man to live with his folks. Don't work out."

"Wouldn't be for always, most likely," said H. A.

"Ain't no Miss Billie Lee back in the sandhills, either." Or Joey Phipps. Or Jimmy Kieffer or Viyella Redfern, as once was.

165

"I know that." H. A.'s eyes didn't see her, straying over her head to the square of black window and darkness beyond.

"Ma, can I make him a birdsong?" Thomas had crept close and laid a hand on her knee.

"When he's through his vittles," Viyella smiled. "Wait a bit." Thomas. She thought of him on the farm, away from folks. He could sing and whittle, she thought, maybe even make things for that Exchange. And if they got some animals!

"Ma." Now Jee Paw came across the room. He was swaggering, his shoulders back, his cowlick bolt upright, standing tall so his brother could see. "I can tote him around for you on my wagon so you won't get so tired."

H. A.'s eyes came back and flew to meet his mother's, but hers never flinched.

"That'll be right kind of you, Jee Paw," she said softly.

"And help fix his bottle."

"You can help right now." Viyella laughed, handing it to him. "Give H. A. a rest." Deftly she swung the baby to her shoulder, her hand supporting his head, and patted his back.

"There's a water tower back there, Jee Paw," she began, but then Woody gave a vigorous, rumbling burp. H. A. grinned and Jee Paw laughed aloud and Thomas lowered his chin, scowling in his effort to imitate. "Oh, no, Thomas! No! One's enough," Viyella scolded, but laughed anyways. "Show it to you someday," she went on, more to herself than them. "Never did want to climb it. But I wish I had."

Jenny Sue would know where to look for them if she came back, Viyella knew. And they could move Fella's stone to lie at home at last.

"Here you go, Woody." She handed him up to H. A., who held him close, his big hand as large as his burden. "Still ain't right, man living with his Ma. Nothing right about it."

166

"Best I can see to do now, Ma, time being. If you're willing."

Her body was still warm where the baby had cradled, and on her shoulder was a spot, sweet-sour, smelling of milk, and her arms were empty.

"Could keep him awhile, maybe, till you find you . . ." She caught her lip between her teeth and her eyes filled. "Maybe move on back for a bit." She could see it and smell it and feel it, all of it: the house set back in the fields, the wisp of smoke from the chimney, the clear blue of the sky above the pines. "Maybe even set out some peach trees yet," she mused. "Mind you, H. A. Just a bit. Just till you're settled, you hear?"

Half the night, Viyella rocked, waiting for Jimmy.

"I'm tired out," she thought. "Already my back aches, and he's but a shoulder baby. Too weary even to move my bones to bed." But the crook of her arm yearned where the baby's head had lain.

And when she heard Jimmy's step on the orange crate, she rose to meet him.

" '*Can*-dy, call my sugar . . .' " he was singing.

"Hush, Jimmy, hush. Don't wake the baby," she began and then stopped herself.

He looked baffled and confused and stood unsteadily leaning against the door frame.

"C'mon Jimmy." Viyella held out her hand to him and led him inside. "C'mon. We're going home."